The People Could Fly

Denise Dragiewicz

"But I'll get back on my feet some day.

The good lord willin', if he says I may.

I'll get up and fly away."

For GD

They say the people could fly. Say that long ago in Africa, some of the people knew magic. And they would walk up on the air like climbin' up on a gate. And they flew like blackbirds over the fields. Black, shiny wings flappin' against the blue up there.

Then, many of the people were captured for slavery. The ones that could fly shed their wings...

The folks were full of misery then...so they forgot about flyin' when they could no longer breathe the sweet scent of Africa.

From *The People Could Fly: American Black Folktales* told by Virginia Hamilton

The Tlingit world was frozen and dark until the young princess Shonee SeeSee sacrificed herself and brought color to the endless winter sky. One day, during the ritual of light, when Shonee SeeSee was doing the traditional snow dance in the middle of the tribe's circle, she became frozen with fear and forgot the steps of the ancient dance. The people all stopped to look at Shonee SeeSee and watched as the joy collapsed inside of her. It was then they knew that Zhouleefunee, the god of death, had come to take Shonee SeeSee's soul to the other side. Panicked, the people tried to scare away Zhouleefunee's spirit and chased the screaming girl through the frozen tundra until she got to the end of an icy precipice and flew away into the winter sky. It was then the Tlingit people first felt grief. Having no protection against this strange emotion, it attacked them like a thousand shards of burning glass raining on their bodies through the winter sky, tearing their clothes and soaking their skin in the colors of blood and tears. Now, their bodies no longer useful to them, their spirits escaped through these colors and entered the sky, determined to find Shonee SeeSee's spirit.

In the winter, when the sun sleeps, the Tlingit people are reminded of their lost princess through all the hours and all the days and all the nights without light, forced to watch Shonee SeeSee's family grieving for all eternity, sometimes alone in solemn shades of emerald green that shoot around in a wandering pattern moving through the glittering stars. Or sometimes they come together to share their grief, and their tears flow out of their woeful souls in a mixture of fuchsias and purples and blues that swirl around inside of the sky, looking for the soul of their lost princess.

"In the story," Dana said, "the girl kills herself because she is being chased by an invisible demon. Then her family grieves for her forever. Her death defines them. Is that what you wanted? To define your family's life by your death? It sounds like revenge. Did you think you could get revenge on your family if you died?"

"Yes. That's what I wanted. I wanted them to know what misery felt like. I wanted my mother to know."

"Is that why you swallowed the bottle of your mother's pain medication, so that she would notice you?"

"Yes, that's why."

Part 1

Lisa

I can hear it already. All the voices huddled in there at the same time. A part of me doesn't want to walk any further. I want to go back to my room and wait until the bus comes.

At my school, a lot of fucked up shit went down in the cafeteria. There was this one really skinny, really dorky looking kid in my junior high that used to sit by himself at lunch because he didn't have any friends, and everybody knew it. John-John, I think his name was, though I'm not sure why people would call him his name two times over. I remember he had these really thick clear braces, but they weren't really clear; they were more like a pukey white color. It was kind of nauseating to look at actually. But he was a nice kid and all. God knows he never did anything bad towards me.

Anyway, there were these boys that used to pick on him pretty badly, especially in the cafeteria, I think because everybody could see, and they would have the audience they were looking for. They would do things like take his milk and pore it over his head.

I remember this one time these two kids, Travis and Cameron, they were having this stupid fucking contest to see who could eat the most hot dogs like they were at a stupid summer carnival or some shit. It seemed like almost everybody from the cafeteria was in on it, and they all went up to get a hot dog so the two boys could get their kicks, and I suppose the crowd wanted theirs as well. Anyway, I don't have to tell you how disgusting it was watching two eighth grade boys pile hot dog after hot dog into their mouths. The whole time I could see them gagging, the two of them. I knew it was gonna come, and at least one of them was gonna puke all over the cafeteria floor. And it was Cameron. I could see it in his face. Everybody could. He just kept heaving and heaving. But he wouldn't let it come out. I remember the crowd chanting, "Go, go, go," as if they wanted him to go on even though it was obvious he was gonna get sick.

But Cameron, he wasn't gonna throw the towel in that quickly and let Travis take all the victory for the day. He had to top it off and make sure he came out on top. And he did. He made his way over to the table all the way up front where little John-John was sitting and minding his own business and finally let himself throw up all over that little guy's head. It was the grossest thing I'd ever seen. And he just kept going and going. Finally, the cafeteria aides came over to break it up. I remember seeing little John-John there, all covered with someone else's throw-up, wiping it off his glasses. He was covered so much he could hardly see, stumbling around all over the place and slipping in it and shit. And all the kids in the cafeteria. You would think they were watching an episode of *Laurel and Hardy*, a classic episode or some shit, by the way that they were laughing. You'd never think it was because of some kid getting puked on.

John-John never did get over that one. The kids at school called him little puke-head or some shit like that till the day he found his way into the safe in his parents' closet and blew his brains out. I remember looking at all those kids that day we found out, all hugging each other and pretending to cry. I just kept thinking, "You have to be kidding me, God. This is the best you could do?"

I stand by the door of the cafeteria, watching all those people in there, and just can't get that day and poor little John-John out of my head, until I feel a little hand come up behind me and wrap itself inside my own. I flinch and pull myself away; then I hear Sara say, "It's just me, silly. Let's get something to eat before they pack up in here. I hear they're only bringing peanut butter and jelly sandwiches on the trip. Yuck."

I never do give Sara back my hand, but I follow her over to the food counter and get some really disgusting overly cooked eggs and a few hash browns from Gloria, the cook, because I know Sara is right, and whatever type of food they're bringing on this stupid little trip we've got going today will probably be much worse than this shit.

About ten minutes into the bus ride, Sara passes out on my left shoulder, and now I'm stuck, kind of uncomfortably, between her head and the cold metal frame of the school bus. She has her arms wrapped around my waist like I'm some type of little doll she used to sleep with at night. She looks too peaceful to wake up, so I just suck it up and stare out the window.

It's beautiful up by the hospital. Sometimes I look out the window, and all I see are trees and trees that blanket the horizon like I'm far away upstate New York or Vermont in the mountains. It must be like your heart can stop up there, and you can slow down and just soak up all that air from those trees. I would love to be around them more often, to wake up and see nothing but trees and know they were really out there, infinitely, as far as I could walk, and people, they were far, far away.

Technically, we're still in the suburbs, so it doesn't take too long to get down to the endless row of shopping malls and residential houses that has become modern-day America. On the way to the parkway, all you see is mini-mall after mini-mall. It's kind of dizzying looking at all that cement and those ridiculous banners advertising all this crap that nobody really needs. That's what we have come to know as home, a land of crap and bullshit things; we spend all our lives working just so we can have them. Isn't that why I'm supposed to go to college, a good college, an expensive college, a business school, that will suck up every last penny my parents have tried to save during a lifetime of bullshit work to force me into spending the next four years of my life in another place I hate, surrounded by people who prostitute themselves to belong to some ridiculous sorority, all around you, pretending, pretending that I like you and you like me, and that one day we'll all make a lot of fucking money and have superficial friends and superficial children and a superficial house that's loaded with a bunch of crap that I don't need and never use, but makes me look good to the neighbors, so I spend all my time and all my energy at some stupid, immoral job that I hate and that's making my blood pressure go through the roof and destroying any sense of morality that I might have had at one time. Meanwhile, I live a sexless life in a loveless marriage with children I never see except when I'm called to the principal's office when they're doing something wrong. But everything in my superficial world looks good on the outside, all a show for others to see, until one day when I'm standing over the grave of my youngest child, who I haven't had a real conversation with in years, and didn't realize she was sleeping with older men for money in order to feed her $1,500 a week heroin habit...

"Lisa. Lisa." I reluctantly look over at Dana to see what she wants now. "We're gonna be there soon. Maybe you should wake Sara up."

"Right."

Sara looks so peaceful when she's asleep. I wonder what goes on in that mind of hers. I wonder if she's able to put it all behind her and go someplace better.

"Sara," I say, but she's out of it. I shake her head a little with my left shoulder, but still she's not responding. So I move the hair away from her face and gently rub her cheek. She's got a beautiful face, Sara. Milky white skin with spots of freckles everywhere. She doesn't belong here with the rest of us. She deserves better than all the crap that's on this earth.

"Oh, I'm up. I'm up," she says with a yawn. "Are we there now?"

"Just about," I tell her. "You can rest for another minute if you want."

When the bus stops, Sara is still trying to pull herself together, so I just wait patiently and watch the others pile off. They're eager to get out. If they're anything like me, it's the first time they've been anywhere in the real world since they were admitted to the hospital. A part of me is apprehensive about getting off this old bus and seeing the real world again with my own eyes. I'm kind of happy on the inside that me and Sara will be the last ones off, so I can pull away and stay far behind.

It's a small little area, very upstate New Jersey, on the border of New York. The trees are still dark and motionless, but it's quiet and subtle and there are rocks all over the place, big boulder rocks that decorate the landscape. I am happy to be here.

I guess today we're breaking up into small groups. Dana gave me a card last night with the letter B on it, and I didn't pay much attention to what it was for, but now I see it's for the fishing group we're supposed to be with for the day. Sara's in group D, and I can tell she's a little nervous about being out here and not being able to stay with me, but I assure her that it's only for a few hours and that when everybody's off fishing, she'll have some time by herself to relax.

There are three other girls in my group, all whom I've never met, but they all give me a smile when I go up to them and politely tell me their names: Jamie, Sienna, and Angela. Down by the river, we get a quick rundown by some park ranger on the ins and outs of fly fishing and how we should handle the pole, which I, for the most part, just blow off since I've been fishing in a river before and don't have any plans of bringing in a twenty pound trout today anyway. About fifteen minutes into our little lecture, the ranger can see that I've had some experience with all this, so he pairs me up with Angela, because it's obvious she's never held a fishing pole in her hands and coordination is not one of her natural talents. I tell her, really, it's just a body motion, and you just have to get into a rhythm of moving your right hand back and then letting the rod jerk forward as quickly as you can. But Angela has a nervous demeanor. She is just like Andrea, but she actually has fully grown nails on her fingertips, so I suppose she hasn't fallen into the same anxious habits. I'm not sure why she is getting so worked up about stupid fly fishing anyway, but she keeps examining every movement I make like there's gonna be some stupid test afterwards.

It's the end of March, but the weather is really kind of nice out today, so I suggest she takes off one of the many layers of clothing she has piled on like she is ready to go on some cross-country ski trip in the Arctic, but Angela says, "No, no, I get cold very easily." She says, "Lisa, if you don't mind, maybe I could just stay back and watch you for a bit. Just give me a little while to watch," and I say, sure, of course. I don't want to force her to do anything she feels uncomfortable doing. In gym class, they would always force me to play volleyball, even though I sucked so badly at it, and I could tell nobody wanted me on their team. I always wished that one of the teachers would just let me hang back and watch. I never saw any point of being forced into doing something you just were no good at. But in school, they always made you do things that you didn't want to do. It's like they got a kick out of watching you humiliated or some shit.

It's kind of nice being out here and fishing all by myself. The funny thing is I think we've been paired up with other people so we can "bond" with them or some other stupid shit, but it's been over an hour, and I've pretty much been out here on my own. Every now and then I throw my head back and ask Angela if she wants to join me, but she usually just says, "Oh no, Lisa, I just want to watch for a little bit more," and I smile and say of course.

I like the water in this river. It's calm and soothing and there aren't many rapids. I bet you I could walk right across it and never have to worry about falling and getting caught up in anything. Not like the ocean. When I was seven, I almost drowned in a rip tide. That was the last time we ever went to the beach. I was out swimming with my sister, April, and when she started playing around with some other girl, I thought it would be fun to swim out a little further, so I could be off by myself for a while. Before I knew it, I was caught in a current that I couldn't get myself out of. I tried and tried to swim back to the shore, but it was no use. No matter what I did, I just kept getting pushed back into the ocean. It was like I was fighting against myself or something. I don't know how long I was out there before the water started to suffocate me, but it felt like a whole lifetime. All I wanted was to find my mother, to paddle my way back to her, to feel the safety of her arms like a life preserver being thrown out to protect me. But I just couldn't do it.

"Lisa. How are you doing? Are you catching anything?" Dana. She can always be counted on to break up any type of private meditation I've been losing myself in.

"No. Nothing's biting."

"How about you, Angela? Having any luck today?"

"No, ma'am. I've just been watching Lisa for a bit. She really knows what she's doing."

"Yes, she's quite the fisherman, or woman, I guess. I didn't know that about you, Lisa. See, I knew there were some special talents you've been keeping from me. Next time you tell me that you're no good at anything, I'm going to remember this moment."

All righty then. She means well, she does, but I just can't think of anything but the word annoying sometimes when she's around.

"You know what would be really special, Lisa?" Oh, yes, here it comes. "If you spent a little time helping Angela, showing her a thing or two, and, Angela, if it's really not for you, then you can sit it out, but I would like to see you spend like ten or fifteen minutes trying. How does that sound?" Dana says with a little manipulative smile planted right in my direction, so I guess I have no choice than to force Angela to take a few whacks at the pole.

So I finally coax her into standing up and promise that I'll only make her give it a shot for a couple of minutes like Dana promised, and I have her stand right inside my arms like my grandfather used to do when he was teaching me how to swing a bat. I position the pole in her hands and have her practice jerking it back and forwards with my arms around it to help with the movements. I know she warned me about getting cold easily and everything, but I say, "Angela, it would really be a lot easier for you to handle the pole if you just take off one of these sweatshirts or at least just roll it up above your elbow."

She just looks up at me and says, "Okay, Lisa. If you really think so," and I nod yes, so she gives me back the pole and rolls up the sleeve on her right arm.

As soon as she starts lifting those layers back, I can tell why she was so adamant about keeping all her clothes on. I've never seen anything so mutilated in my entire life as the arm on that girl. I'm confused, and I guess I do something that I shouldn't have. I grab a hold of that arm and just start looking and looking at it. "Angela, what happened?" I say. "Who did this to you?"

"No one," she says in a soft voice I could hardly hear. "I did it to myself."

And I can't help but ask her, "Why would you do that to yourself like that? It looks like it hurts something awful. Was it some type of accident?"

"No," she says. "It just makes me feel better. That's why I do it."

TWO

A jackhammer buzzes in the distance. I don't know where it's coming from. When I look out the window, all I see are branches of sleeping trees, still and eloquent. They sleep patiently through the winter, soaking in the quiet. I look at them and think of the Northern Pole where everything is motionless and become envious.

The air is dull and hazy. There is a twilight grayness to it. Besides that jackhammer, there is quiet all around. It makes me calm inside, like a picture I once saw of Tibetan monks meditating in the early dawn with the curvy backdrop of the Himalayas. I remember that picture, from a world history class. It's one that always stayed with me. There were hundreds of them, dressed in their burgundy robes, all sitting there, legs crossed, eyes shut, hands lifted in prayer. And the mountains all around them. I bet you the air in those mountains feels sterile and uncorrupted. I close my eyes, and I can almost feel it entering my lungs. I remember those long, deep breaths from yoga and want to be still and patient like those monks, my head quiet and empty, my breath steady and hypnotizing. Here I am not frozen. I am in the quiet of the mountains. There are birds, like the Kashmir flycatcher with calming shades of browns and oranges. They fly above me as I sit in stillness with my mind uninhibited, just those mountains and the unsoiled air that cannot soak in quick enough. The birds, I hear their songs drifting in the blue. I am one with the monks, quiet and peaceful and centered. The birds sing, "Lisa, you are free. You can let go."

I'm almost lost in the memory of this picture, till I hear that jackhammer buzzing again, then a nurse walking in the hallway, dropping one of those metal clipboards. I hear her say, "Oh, fuck," outside my door, and then the loose shuffling of papers being thrown back into that clipboard. It is about seven o'clock now anyway, and the others will begin to get up. Today there is an old woman coming to talk about survival. She was a young German girl during World War II, and her family was murdered at Auschwitz. Somehow, she survived. I think this is Dana's idea, another trick up her sleeve to manipulate me, to show me how bad other people have had it, but yet they went on. They wanted to live. They were almost desperate for it. That should make me feel what, envious? Or perhaps it should make me feel guilty. What an ungrateful brat I must be to have thrown in the towel so eagerly, praying for death instead of fighting for life. This woman, she's supposed to make me feel better or worse, I'm not sure.

That camp she was at during the war, Auschwitz, we learned about in high school, in another one of those history classes. I remember the pictures: the yellowness of the walls, the bricks, the chains, the poison in the showers. It was a place people were brought to die. I remember feeling I could be like one of those Jews. I looked around and knew I was trapped within those same decaying walls, poison leaking out of the little pores in the stone bricks, faintly creeping into you, slowly affecting your brain, numbing you, forcing you into passivity; the insidiousness of the poison working its magic on the unsuspecting students, all moving with the flow of the crowd, latching onto the familiar. It takes a year or two for the poison to embed deeply enough into the bloodstream; the body begins to feel faint and paralyzed. One more year, and the lungs begin to freeze. You gasp for breath, but it's never enough. You walk around choking, coughing up blood. You look to others with your hands pressed desperately to your chest, trying to speak, faintly panting, "Help me, help me," with the pale energy that your body has retained. But the others around you, drone-like, are only able to fixate on what is directly in front of their eyes, always looking ahead at something that can never be attained. And so, with the oxygen you have left quickly dwindling, you collapse, unable to take one step further; but your eyes remain open, and you watch as the others keep passing, stepping over your lifeless body, tripping over your unresponsive limbs.

"Lisa, are you still sleeping in there? It's 7:30. Time to get up," says that same nurse, Jackie, who was stumbling outside my door a half hour ago. Getting us all up in the morning is the last duty of her shift. She will leave at 8:00 am sharp. She is a young nurse, goofy and ridiculous and arriving on the doorstep of this old house minutes after the pomp and circumstance of her community college graduation. "This is the only stupid job I could get," she tells her old high school friends who are equally making little money and living at home with mom and dad. I know all about this nurse. I hear her talk outside my window all night long as she takes incessant smoking breaks every half hour. The other nurse who shares her shift does not share her same enthusiasm for smoking and only accompanies her two or three times throughout the night. But Jackie likes to keep herself on the edge and relies on an unremitting diet of nicotine and caffeine to push her through her shifts. I hear her talking on her overpriced cell phone when she takes these cigarette breaks. She talks to her friend Pamela, "Pammy," until she goes to sleep at about two in the morning. Then she goes to her ex-boyfriend Timothy who has moved to the west coast to explore an acting career. From about two to three in the morning, I hear her say, "I miss you so much, baby. I wish you would come home, and we could get back together. I would make you happy. I promise," in a sophomoric, pathetic voice. When she's with us, she is as stern and as rigid as my elementary school principal who worked too long after her retirement deadline and liked to tell us stories of living off bread and potatoes in the early

40s. "In those days, girls could only get an education till the eighth grade. Then we had to stay home and tend to our little brothers and sisters. You don't know how lucky you have it to be able to go all the way through high school." I often thought of that woman, looking around for little knives I could carry in my bag, just in case, at some random moment, I would gather the strength to finally cut my body in some morbid way. I would think about her foreboding words that were supposed to inspire me.

Jackie is young, probably no more than twenty-two or twenty-three, but she wears those same circular eye glasses that my old principal used to wear and speaks to us in the same drowned-out, artificial voice as that old woman who missed the days when teachers could walk around with ruler sticks. Only I know that this stern voice of hers is merely a mirage of power within her minute, ineffective world. "Lisa, if you don't get up now, you're going to miss breakfast, and I'll have to write it down in your folder," she warns.

"Coming," I say. "Just getting dressed," I yell through the doorway, though I'm still lying in bed with little intention of rushing out any time soon. She will leave in two minutes anyway, at exactly eight am, and the other nurse who will take her place has little concern for formality, so I am not worried about missing breakfast or receiving some type of demerit in my folder.

Her hands hold the wheel firmly as her eyes look side to side, monitoring the street in front of her. She never looks back, but I look to her eyes anyway. I hope that my stare into her rearview mirror will break her concentration on the road in front of her, and she will turn around to inquire about the girl who is crying on the bus.

Probably ten aisles back, they sit, plotting their next move when the bus stops in a few minutes, thinking if they can catch me before I reach my house. If not, there is morning at the bus stop. They can make up something creative by then.

"Why would you want to hurt your mother, Lisa?"

"Because she doesn't love me."

"Why do you think she doesn't love you?"

"Because she ignores me."

"How does she ignore you, Lisa?"

"She sees me crying all the time. She always did, and she never asks me why. She never does anything about it. She just lets me stay in my room and cry."

"She never asks you what's wrong?"

"No, she doesn't care. And I hate her. She should have helped me, but she didn't. She could've taken me away from that school before Josh and Paul...before they made me so miserable. But she didn't. I asked her, and she said no. They didn't have the money. But that was a lie. They have the money. I know they do. They bought my sister a new car. A new fucking car. But she wouldn't send me to Catholic school. She just looked at me like I was too weak to suck it up. Like I should handle my own problems. But she was my mother. She should have helped me."

Allison

The last couple of nights, I walk into the bathroom at my usual time, and Allison's all naked with her shit sprawled out all over the place. There are about five individual showers in that bathroom, all with their own stalls to do whatever shit you need to accomplish in that space, but Allison insists on walking around that whole bathroom showing off that little plastic razor they just trusted her to hold for fifteen minutes while someone comes in and out to make sure she doesn't take that little blade off that piece of plastic it's attached to. It is a "privilege" to shave your legs in this place, but, of course, it comes with regulations. That bitch nurse Jackie has to sit out there and monitor every little thing you do while you have a few minutes alone to clean yourself. And my few minutes alone just became obsolete, not only with Allison, but also that stuck up young nurse that gets under my skin like a splinter.

"Everything all right in there?" she says, walking in and sizing up Allison to make sure she's doing everything she's supposed to be doing.

"Oh yeah, Jackie, doing fine. Just making sure I'm getting all the parts I need to get. Haven't had myself a razor in so long I've almost forgotten what I want to keep and what I want to get rid of," she says, looking over at me with a little wink, which kind of makes my stomach turn. "I'm just about finished here. Just give me another five to finish up and pull my shit together."

"All right, Allison. That's about all you have, so hurry up. And Lisa, it's ten to nine. I don't have to remind you that your time is falling short as well, do I?"

There always has to be some obnoxious comment. I can read the fucking clock that's right up there on the wall staring me in the face. "Of course, Jackie. I'll only be a sec," I say and try to keep my eyes straight, so I don't roll them in her face. If she knows you're talking back to her, she'll be on your ass like a teacher trying to keep you from cheating, and then everything will be coupled with the comment, "I'll have to write that in your folder," like we're inmates who have to go in front of a parole board. She's that fucking insecure, and it's so transparent in almost a clichéd type of way.

Seeing as she's naked, it's almost difficult not to stare. Allison's got stupid tattoos in too many places on her emaciated, stringy body, you would think she was trying to make some political statement with hackneyed, bullshit testimonials she read on the Internet. And most of them are so badly done it looks like one of her druggie friends drew on her skin with some washed out Magic Marker attached to a little motor they bought at a convenience store. I would be embarrassed if I was her, but for some stupid reason, I can see that she is proud of them.

The temperature had risen to over 104 degrees that July afternoon. After nightfall, long after it had cooled off, a young, white, suburban, middle-class male from an average-sized American town somewhere about forty miles north of Philadelphia, on the New Jersey border, brought his wife to the hospital to give birth to their second child. It was late, between two and three in the morning, when she began to feel sudden pains on the sides and bottom of her stomach, and before she could lean over to shake her husband out of a deep sleep, the woman's body excreted so much fluid, so suddenly and in such a large quantity, it felt like somebody popped a large balloon filled with liquid only a little heavier than water, right between her legs. It was then she knew it was a girl; only the gentleness of a female spirit could wake her up so innocently, with this quiet announcement, so lightly it felt like a whisper, when the baby thought it was time to make her way into the world.

The boy had been very different. Constant, vibrating attacks along the bottom part of her spine had made a home inside her body at the end of the fourth month of her first pregnancy and decided to stay until the ninth month, until the angry baby made up its mind to leave. This was the experience of her first child, Nicholas II.

Her second child, though, the girl, only gave her mother a gentle nudge in the middle of the night to let her know it was time to go to the hospital.

Allison sometimes tries to remember herself through the stories she hears her mother telling friends and relatives after evenings of wine and after-dinner cordials at holiday get-togethers—she, as a baby, always smiling, always quiet, her mother always able to "bring her anywhere," and she would run around, playfully, happily, in her walker with the rolling wheels, sucking on her teething toys, smiling at whoever smiled back. She cannot remember playing with her brother when she was very young, but she can imagine their differences through these stories—her mother's voice always grew louder and louder, almost like it would reach a peak and then snap, when telling of Nicholas. But with Allison, her voice got soft and easy. Boys run around the house breaking memories and souvenirs with basketballs that were only meant for outside, but girls, to her mother, especially her Allison, play quietly in their bedrooms with plastic dolls and pretend houses, all day and all night, so quietly that her mother, sometimes, would run in a panic from across the house, scared that perhaps her child had choked and stopped breathing while she was off, not paying attention. Allison, who always ate vegetables and drank milk, and didn't have to be bribed with dessert to finish dinner, was unlike her brother who would spit his broccoli into a napkin and then stamp his feet and throw a tantrum when his mother refused to give him ice cream after an unfinished meal.

Allison does not remember all these fond moments that her mother shares, but she's been listening to them as far back as she can remember, and each time, each one of these stories that she overheard made her think she was listening to the story of another girl's life, because she never believed that others could think of her in such an easy way.

She's in bed now and remembering her mother's touch. But these memories cannot transform into feelings, into the actual sensation of her mother's cool, clammy hands holding her warm forehead, rubbing smooth fingers back through her sweaty hair. In her memory, her mother is holding her from behind, one hand on her forehead, close to the hairline, the other hand rubbing the tense muscles in her shoulder, as Allison leans over the toilet, an eight-year-old with a stomach flu.

Now, there is no mother or warm body to lean against, only a hard mattress smelling of sickness, blankets that have been washed too many times, but do not retain that comfortable worn out feeling of old cotton. She lays her head flat on the bed without the pillow, staring at the walls she has just noticed, with her head lying sideways, walls without pictures, old yellow walls with peeling paint dripping down like decoration, but no memories of love hanging on them.

Outside of these thoughts, the only feeling that moves her away from the nausea is the constant pulsing of her left leg, that she cannot control, the one she is using to hold down her right. Vomit will no longer come out of her throat; there is no more vomit inside to release the disgust being held like a tight cramp inside of her

Denise Dragiewicz

body. *All she knows now are muscle jerks and stomach flus that are worse than stomach flus, worse than poisoning that slowly creeps inside hours after eating food on winter trips to Mexico; now it is only vomit that is no longer there, except embedded in the lining of her mouth and through the senses of her nose. It is not like the first time she did heroin. Then, the nausea was brief and the comfortable feeling of her mother's arms around her when she was sick could not contend with the calm pleasure she experienced in that first moment of her new life.*

That liquid left a silky feeling sliding through her vein like her feet playing under the comfort of old sheets on Sunday mornings, when she didn't have to wake up. Just the feeling of lying there, alone, doors closed, house sleeping, stomach still content from dinner the night before. In the mornings with no alarm clocks, no school buses, no soccer games, she would lie in her quiet bedroom and rub her legs up and down underneath her own sheets that were clean, but old and worn in, and silky smooth like the heroin she would come to love years later that would instead slide underneath her skin and leave her again with the comfortable feeling of worn out sheets on Sunday mornings.

That is what she misses. Her old bed and the old sheets she wouldn't let her mother replace. She never knew that protected, comfortable feeling again after she left that house. And after they left Tristan's apartment, that secure, quiet feeling of closed doors in a private home would become another thought she could only try to

38

remember.

On a warm, early winter afternoon, a few days before or after the start of a new school quarter, Allison got off a bus in Philadelphia and understood what others would only know through newspaper stories or movie fiction; others, who could only imagine a homeless teenager begging for money with a paper cup or leaning over a reclined window trying to sell a blow job for less than twenty bucks, were now the ones who were far removed from Allison's life. Those thoughts she tried to pull into her present mind of comfortable mothers or quiet bedrooms became distant memories that were glazed over, hidden through the foggy life of an addict, muffled through weeks and months of constant drugs and nights that drifted too quickly into morning.

Then, feeding took on a different form, but it was feeding just the same. It kept her quiet and still; always waiting for the guy to drop off the stuff she really wanted. Hours would crawl by in the time waiting for him, and when finally her thoughts drifted towards food, she would hear a knock on the door that instantly replaced that hunger.

Lying in her hospital bed, she hears sirens, sirens, all the time outside windows that are covered shut, making the memories of when the police came running down the block in lines of screaming cars heading towards Tristan's apartment real again. Too early in the morning in stores that weren't closed, she watched the cars run down the block, as she gave quarters to bums while

Tristan bought beer inside. He walked out the door soon enough to watch the last car speed by in the echo of the ten in front of it. Now the beer didn't matter, and he grabbed her hand and started running through the bushes of neighbors' houses.

It was Tristan they wanted, but she was with him just the same and didn't know where else to go, so even as he let go of her hand and started running almost too quickly for her to keep up, she kept as close as she could behind him and followed him all the way to the bus stop leading towards the city. Waiting for the bus, hiding behind the thinly ripped ads stuck in pieces to the dirty Plexiglas of the bus stop, she couldn't hear any sounds except the sirens in the distance, and Tristan's constant panic—"Fuck, fuck, fuck, we're fucked, we're fucked."

This was confusing for her, but Tristan was the only thing she knew. He was the only direction she knew how to follow.

All of those consequences that Allison never considered when she watched Tristan stuffing money into secret places, old vents and unzipped couches, now stood there waiting with them in the minutes at the bus stop, listening to the sirens through the tranquil streets, from the direction of his apartment complex. Her eyes would take turns looking for people behind her, to the nothingness on the floor below her, to looking at his face in quick snaps, for some assurance, but all she saw was fear. His face never looked so yellow and so sickly as it did when he thought about those policemen at his apartment searching through the inventory of his narcotics, talking in elevated voices about the years they could "put this kid away," too many for him to think about. No, now, it was only Philadelphia where he could melt into the anonymity of the other street kids, the ones the police would want just as badly.

The bus isn't there yet, and they begin to hear the sirens fading in the background. Allison's body starts to shake in a way she never felt before, but she tries to keep it all inside, holding back the throw-up that was starting to find its way outside of her stomach, so as not to embarrass herself, afraid that Tristan would slip away from her if he feels she will make them lose their obscurity.

When it finally came, he walked them right to the back of the bus and pulled his cap over his head, pretending to fall asleep, with only the constant movement of his knees popping up and down making it obvious that he wasn't. Now, briefly, she thinks about the police looking through all of her things in his apartment, her pocketbook and her school ID, paying close attention to the details of her features, her shoulder length blonde hair or aqua colored eyes. Then she thinks about where they are going and the thought of it being without drugs replaces any of the old fear she had of the police and her photo ID.

Her hand tightly holds the cold metal bar of the bus to help her avoid the dizziness that comes and goes as the bus jerks forward and then back again, and every time her nose moves closer to the bar, she remembers angel dust, the smell of burning window cleaner, smoked in a clay pipe in the shape of a peace sign, that brought

Tristan into her life, when he was the new kid at their school over a year ago. That smell would escape most of the ninth grade, but it was familiar to him, and she liked that. This familiarity was more important to her than the sweetness of his eyes or the softness of his hair or the easiness of his style that made him instantly popular with the other girls in her grade.

As her eyes move towards the carpet-less floor of the hospital room, she remembers waking up in Philadelphia at five in the morning, light creeping in through the lines of the curtains, unable to move her body, pain from her temples vibrating down into the bones of her face. She knows it is not just the cement she slept on or the food that wasn't in her stomach, because she cannot get up, the right side of her body paralyzed, without any sensation. The room inside was quiet, everybody sleeping, and Allison was just lying there, facing the window, looking at the tiny beads of light through the curtains that kept getting brighter and brighter; morning was coming, and she couldn't feel the side of her body that was lying against the cement, on the carpet that almost wasn't there, that she must have closed her eyes on top of, the last time she fell asleep.

Every memory of fear comes back to her all at once as her mind focuses on her body paralyzed on the floor. Her pulse pumps hard through every artery. She cannot catch her breath and wants to cry but is too panicked for the tears to come. She can only sit there, silent and feeling her body pump in areas she wished did not exist.

Then, fear turns into blame. She did that to herself. If she never felt movement in her body again, it was her fault and hers alone. She tries, but she cannot remember the last time she ate, even a chocolate bar, and in the process of trying to remember, her mind must have been triggering stomach muscles, and she was no longer numb; instead, everything was becoming acute and real, and for the first time in months, she was living in the present.

"God, if you let me get up, I'll change. I'll get clean. I'll be different. Please. I'll change. I swear. Please, God, please. Let me have another chance." And when her prayers are answered, a damp pinching sensation begins to move through the tips of her fingers and the bottoms of her toes, getting more and more intense, pins and needles throughout her body, and her mind starts drifting more and more away from God and more and more towards the drugs that might be left in somebody else's pocket.

She pauses and considers her options. Maybe she could walk out of that motel room and find a clinic or any other place to get help, even call her parents, anything; so many ideas, so many options, come to her, but they too soon become fantasy-like delusions as she breathes in the scent of fresh smoke and reaches out her hand to take the joint that is being passed in her direction.

"Hey, girl. Check out this one I got here on my back. It's my latest one. It means 'Free your mind' in Sanskrit. I became friends with this guy Louie when I was living in downtown Philly, and he slid it to me for nothing. I think he wanted a little something more, if you know what I mean, but I just kept it platonic. He was a bit too old for me, like in his forties or something, and I thought, you know, I think I'm gonna scale back and stay out of that mid-life range for now. I've got plenty of time to explore that area later on," she tells me with a little wink out of her left eye, which I suppose she thinks she's trademarked in some way, cause I don't think I've ever been within ten feet of Allison without her trying to swing that little gesture in my direction.

"It's cool, Allison. I like it," I tell her, even though it's the most pathetic excuse for a tattoo I've ever seen.

"You should get one too, Lisa. Lots of people will do it even though you're not eighteen. We'll think of something special for you, and I'll set you up with someone I know."

"Sure, that sounds great," I say and try to move myself quickly out of this moronic conversation before the brain cells in my head start fading away. It's fucking seven to nine. If I don't get into the shower soon, I'm gonna get stuck on line in the morning, waiting around with too many other conversations I'm not in the mood to get into.

"You should get something written out in some Sioux Indian type of language or something like that. You know, I've

44

read a lot about those Indians, and they got a lot of spiritual sayings to them and stuff."

"Sure, Allison. Think of something cool for me. That sounds great," I say as I grab my stuff and quickly find my way into the shower with only moments waiting on the clock. But she still won't give it up even with the faucet turned on and steam rising out of the stall.

"You know who also has a lot of deep sayings, Lisa? The Greeks. I bet you we could get a book on that. What da ya say, tomorrow, we head down to the library and look for something? What da ya say, Lisa?"

Oh my God. The bitch is never gonna give it up. "Yes, Allison," I scream from the shower. "We'll do it tomorrow." Anything to shut her up and make her go away.

And then I hear Jackie come in. "Okay, Allison. It's time to go now."

"Right. Lisa. I'll catch you later, and we can talk," she screams as she's being pushed out the door by Jackie, the one redeeming thing I've seen that nurse do since I've been here.

"And Lisa, you have about three minutes. Don't make me come back for you next."

"Be right out, Jackie," I say with a little extra depth to my voice, just to make extra sure that she can hear me.

And there's that. This is the third night in a row I've had to deal with that bullshit, and now I'm gonna have to think about any other time I could possibly slip in here on my own. It's one of the only moments I have all to myself besides late at night when everyone is sleeping, and I'm not going to let them take it from me.

I walk out in the hall with about thirty seconds remaining on the clock and see Jackie waiting for me. She has a subtle look of disappointment cause I made it out by the deadline, and now she's gonna have to look a little harder to find something juicy to write down in that notepad of hers. And I just look over at her like she was doing me a favor cause I know for some reason a little look like that is all it takes to get underneath her skin.

Andrea

No one's around, so I start roaming the hallway, hoping I'll find some way to amuse myself, when I see the other overnight nurse, Margot. "Everybody's in the rec room watching a movie, Lisa. Why don't you go and join them," she tells me, nudging me in that direction. I guess she doesn't want me roaming the hallways by myself, and this is her delicate way of telling me so. Whatever. I'm sure whatever ridiculous thing they have playing will soon be over anyway.

There are about ten girls in the rec room, and they're so glued to the television they don't even notice when I come in. They have some really pathetic movie on with Lindsay Lohan. I remember when it came out, and, trust me, I didn't rush out to the theaters. They're all so involved with it though, as if it's telling them some important truth about life. But this is the world we live in now, so absent of anything that could possibly stimulate your mind in some constructive way. No wonder why I'm so disinterested in everything. And people make it seem like it's my fault, like I have some personal issues because life is so stupid. I remember when I was in junior high my mother tried extra hard to get me to sign up for cheerleading. She thought it would be good for me, like I could practice it throughout high school and make friends. Make friends with whom, I would tell her. Are those really the people you want me to make friends with? But she didn't get it. To her, I was just being dramatic.

Andrea, she was talking the other day about cheerleading and how that's one thing she always wanted to do but never did, and Dana's all like well you still can; there's still time. I'm sorry, but the girl's a high school dropout. What time does she really have? Even if she decides to finish, she's only gonna be able to get her GED. Her cheerleading days are over, and I think it's rather irresponsible of Dana to try to get her hopes up like that, when it's obviously never gonna happen. I suppose if she wanted she could focus on other things, but all I ever do hear her talking about are boys, which, I'm sorry, I don't see as being very productive either.

The other day in group, Dana's all like asking us serious shit like, "Is there anything from your past that you feel you have gotten over, but, perhaps, you really haven't gotten over?" and looking right at me, but I just turned my eyes away and started circling the room. It was too early to start digging down that deep, especially to a bunch of strangers, but Andrea can always be counted on to pick up that baton and start spilling her guts about some stupid shit I can never make sense of.

It's only about ten past nine, and I can tell I'm not the only one that's not in the mood for this shit. We all just sit there in silence for about three minutes straight. Dana's being all patient with us, probably inside thinking in some therapeutic way she's doing the right thing, letting us all sit there and be introspective and shit. Sorry to burst her bubble, but I'm just sitting around looking at this godforsaken wall art they got in this stupid rec room. There are tacky, worn out posters all over the place of "fun" things to do at the Jersey Shore. Ferris Wheels and crab cakes and little kids playing in the sand with plastic buckets. Is that supposed to cheer us up? I haven't met one person in this entire fucked up place that's come from a happy family, except possibly Amanda and her mother's dead anyway, so why the hell would we want to look at images like that, images of things we don't have and never will. I can't imagine it doing anything other than making people feel worse than they already do.

"Yes, Andrea, did you want to go first?"

Oh, here we go. And I can't think of nothing in my head to zone out on for the next hour and forty-five minutes.

"I wanted to have a baby," she says with her fingers in her mouth already. And the rest of us all look up and snap out of whatever daydream we've been abiding in. The girl's only sixteen. And that's been the biggest regret of her life.

"What do you mean by that, Andrea?" Dana asks.

"I mean, I wanted to have a baby, last year, but Bobby

wouldn't let me. He said, 'No, Andrea, you're too young, and I don't have the money. Maybe in a few years from now. Then we'll talk about it.' But I didn't want to wait a few years. I was all alone in New York City. He worked all day and really didn't like me going out without him, so all I did was sit around in our small apartment and watch television. You know, you watch those shows during the day, and everyone has a baby, and they look so happy, and I thought I would want one too, and even though he said we weren't ready, I knew he would be happy if he found out I was pregnant, so I decided I would stop taking my birth control pills."

And now we're all glued to this little monologue like we're watching it unravel on daytime television. Even Dana, I can tell she wants to hear every juicy little tidbit, even though she's trying to hide it and act all conservative.

"Yeah, girl, go on with it. Tell us what happened," Allison throws in, cause we can all see that Andrea's hesitating just a little bit. She's taken to biting off real pieces of flesh on the tip of her right index finger and letting it dribble down her mouth.

Dana's not even telling her to stop. All she can say is, "Go on, Andrea; it's okay."

"Well, three months later, I stopped getting my period, and that was it. Now I just had to tell Bobby. But I couldn't. I waited for months and months, and, finally, I just did it. We were watching this show at night, and there was this girl, and she was telling her man the same thing, and he looked so happy. Bobby was just sitting there next to me, kind of snuggling me on the couch, acting so nice and all, and so I thought, Andrea, this is the time. Tell him now," and then Andrea just sat back and retreated, looking scared, like she didn't want to go any further.

"Yeah, Andrea, you can't stop now. You have to tell us what happened next."

"Okay, Allison, she'll go on when she can. I don't think it's a good idea for us to rush her. Andrea, it's okay, take your time," Dana tells her, and now it's burning in all of us to find out what happened next, although it's obvious she doesn't have a child.

"Well," Andrea says, and looks around at all of us, digging those fingers deeper into her mouth. "He wasn't happy," and she pauses again. "He got all mad and crazy and started throwing things around the room and stuff. He said I was a bitch and that I was trying to trap him. And he went through all my stuff and found the birth control pills that I wasn't taking and everything. It was really bad. I don't think anything that meant anything to me made it through that night. He just went though the whole apartment and smashed everything. Even two of my teeth fell out. We had to go to the emergency room at 5:00 in the morning and everything cause my mouth just wouldn't stop bleeding. See these two front teeth right here," she says, holding up her lip and tapping her middle finger on her two fake teeth like she was showing off a trophy. It was so weird. She was trying to skate around the issue that Bobby had hit her so hard that her teeth broke off and fell out, but it was so obvious, even if she didn't want to admit it in real, non-fiction terminology.

"And then what happened to the baby, Andrea, what did you do?"

And she just looks at us with those fingers in her mouth, staring out like she's afraid to tell. "Well, nothing happened, I guess. Two days later Bobby took off of work for the day, and we went down to see a doctor."

"And then what?" I said, even though I was trying not to be nosey.

"And that was it. There was no more baby. Bobby said I had to get rid of it. And the doctor said it might not be easy seeing as it was in the second trimester and all, and he said maybe I should rethink it and all, but all the time he's telling us that Bobby's holding my hand hard underneath the table, as if to say don't even think about it or you're gonna get it later. And I just say no to the doctor. I gotta do it. I can't have the baby. Please understand. And I wanted to cry so hard right then and there, but that hand of Bobby's was keeping all of that inside, cause I knew if I let everything out right there in the doctor's office that we would go back to the apartment later on, and he would break everything else that hadn't been broken before, so I just held everything in and went with the nurse to fill out the paperwork and two days later that was it. It was over. The baby was gone."

"And what did it feel like, girl? My friend Suzy, I went with her down to the clinic once to help her do the same thing except she didn't have a man. I don't think she even knew where the baby was coming from to begin with, but that's another story. Anyway, she was crying and bleeding and cramping up something awful for days and days. It made me think I was never gonna forgo using a condom in the heat of passion ever again."

"Okay, Allison, thank you for your input, but it's still Andrea's turn to talk, and I think she might want to finish on her own."

"It's okay, Dana. I don't mind. She's right. It did hurt. The doctor warned me it might be even worse than it usually is for other girls seeing as I waited so long and everything, and it was. I never knew so much blood could come out of my body. And it just kept coming. Days later, I had to go back to the hospital because they said I was hemorrhaging. It was so bad when I got there the doctors said if I waited any longer, I would have probably bled to death. I never thought about that happening. I just kept thinking about my baby when I saw all that blood, that it was my baby dying and that was all her blood coming out. I just stayed there at home in the middle of all those bloody sheets for days and cried and cried. I don't know where Bobby had gone. He went to work one day and didn't come home till three days later. That's when I went to the hospital.

In the back of the room, there is a bright light and something moving in the background against the reflection of a silver mirror. It is a young woman getting dressed, leaning her right leg over a padded ottoman and rolling up a pair of stockings. Over the stockings, the woman puts on a tight fitting pink nylon bodysuit. She has a beautiful face and a petite frame. Her brown hair is twirled up neatly into a tight fitting round bun. After she is dressed, she re-applies black mascara, darkens circles with a brown liner around her squinting eyelids, and rubs her lips to get the gloss on smooth and tight. One more look in the mirror, and then she quickly runs to the stage.

Her hand shakes as she reaches to turn the brass knob on the wooden door; she pauses for a moment, but there is a light glow and a faint smile sharing the room on her overly decorated face. Seventeen-year-old Diana will dance tonight, for the first time, in the New York City Ballet, as a student in their classical dancing academy.

Too soon it is fall again, but this year the leaves are heavy and dark and the rain has caused the trees to shed too soon. Diana has just given birth to her first baby, Michele, named after the mistletoe she met her first husband Darryl underneath. Eighteen years old and a baby and no more dancing school. Too soon Darryl begins to work too hard and drink too much. Then he gets mad at Diana for too many reasons, and his fists start to hit her in too many places. She stays and stays in their small, barely furnished apartment that he won't let her out of, all alone with just a crying baby and no more dreams and no more dancing, just little broken bones and eyes that are so tired and puffy they cannot cry any more tears, until one day, when she has to leave. He hits her too hard. Then he picks her up and throws her on the kitchen floor. She cannot move, and Darryl can tell her shoulder has fallen out of its socket. Diana begins to cry heavy tears, and Darryl feels sorry. "I'm sorry. I'm sorry," he says. "Let me take you to the hospital." So he keeps his promise and picks Diana up and puts her in his car. Then he remembers the baby Michele and puts her in the backseat.

At the hospital, the nurse knows what happened. She wants to help. She says Diana and the baby can leave and go to a special home. Darryl will never know. He will never find them. They can help Diana get a divorce. "I don't know. I don't know," she says. "He's the baby's father. He's sorry. Never again, he promised." But the nurse says, "No, no, he's not sorry. He will do it again. He will hurt you and then the baby. You have to go, now." And before Diana could think about what she wanted, the nurse was rushing her and Michele out the back entrance of the hospital where Darryl couldn't see. A secret car brought them to a secret place with other young girls with blackened eyes and broken bones and little children that were too small and too scared. And Diana stayed there for a couple of months until the baby could crawl and a paper came in the mail that said now she was single again, no longer married, so she could leave and start again and find a new husband who would give her another baby and eyes that were blacker and little bones that were more broken than they were before.

Five

In the corner of the rec room, I sit, pushing wooden chips around an empty Scrabble board. Amanda and Andrea are playing cards by the couch. We're supposed to be "communicating," but we're off by ourselves doing pointless, random crap. Allison's by the window rambling about nonsense, playing her usual game, trying to get attention in any way she can. I watch her sitting in the corner, staring at that middle finger of hers, rubbing it up and down her greasy forehead. She's been sitting like that for twenty minutes, her eyes fixated only on that hand in front of her face like a madman who's about to snap.

In my lackluster imagination, I watch her chasing little kids around the playground for their lunch money. And getting her eight-year-old kicks out of it.

"Hey, Lisssaaahhh, why are you over there playing with yourself like that?" she says, pointing her greasy finger at me. "Hey, come over here. Yes, you, come, come." And I stare, a little confused and a little pissed. Allison, and her psychotic little mood swings, is the last thing I want to deal with at this time in the morning.

I just look in the other direction and bite on my fingernails, like I can't understand her from so far away.

I close my eyes and concentrate on the strong, definite beat of the circle clock. The seconds pass by, loud and emphatic. But my life remains motionless, plain and dull and mixed up and disorganized like the board game I can't figure out how to play. Bergen State Psychiatric Institution. That's what it all boils down to. The culmination of my sixteen years. And now I just sit here and wait. Playing an outdated board game with the boredom of my own company, listening to old clocks beat away, reminding me how trivial and meaningless it all is.

My eyes shift around the room, still heavy from my morning medication. I look over by the door and think about running. I wonder how far I would get. I wonder if anyone would care enough to come after me.

There's a man over there, looking intently at the glass windowpanes in the door, as if he's contemplating deeply whether or not to come in. From far away, all I see is his bleachy hair, uncombed and uncared for, an apparition waving in and out of my subconscious. He nonchalantly walks through the door, sizing up the features in the room. I wonder if he is just a figment of my imagination. And if so, how far my imagination will let me play this one out.

"Haven't been here in years," he says, looking intently at the dated, old paintings. "The walls used to be more of an orange color. I liked that better."

"Say you over there," he says, turning around and pointing to Andrea. "Fix me the usual, a gin fizz. I always loved the limes in this place. The freshest I've ever tasted."

He walks closer to the table where Andrea and Amanda are playing cards, shuffling through his pockets as he makes his way. "Hey Sam, it looks like I'm clear out for the day. You don't mind spotting me a bit or two, do you?" His eyes fixated on Andrea as if he's talking to an old friend.

And she stares back. Part of her apprehensive, I can tell, but the other part wants him to keep coming towards her. And he does. He sits down at the table, then picks up the cards and begins to shuffle.

"I remember these," he says. "Used to use this same set over at the canteen. Gin Rummy. No one could beat me. I was the crown winner."

"Hey, mister," Allison says. Then she gets up and walks over. "What'cha doing here? I think you may have stumbled into the wrong building."

"No, that's just fine. I know where I am. Just haven't been around in a while. I remember you, Ethel. Say, what did you do with your hair? You used to be so pretty. Everybody couldn't keep their eyes from you. You could go back to that, you know, if you wanted."

"I don't know what you're talking about, mister. I've had this look for years. And my name ain't Ethel."

"Hey, honey," he says, pulling her in closely by the arm. "You don't have to be afraid of so many things."

"I ain't afraid of nothing, mister. I say you're in the wrong place," she exclaims and pulls herself away from him.

But he just looks back at Andrea and Amanda and continues to shuffle the cards. "Hey, Sam. I'm gonna deal for the day. How's that gin fizz coming?"

"You can have my Coke, sir," Amanda says with a nervous demeanor, sliding over her can of soda. "We don't have any gin."

"Flat out. I remember those days. We used to make it in the old basement."

And the two of them sit quietly and listen to his stories of bootlegged liquor and the Great Depression, holding onto the cards he just shuffled like Rummy was a game they knew how to play.

But Allison, shifting her eyes back and forth in a tenuous, resentful manner, quickly moves in. "Hey, mister. You're not supposed to be in here. You gotta get going, or I'm gonna call a guard."

"Oh, Ethel," he just says, turning around to look at her. "Always complaining about something, aren't you? Why don't you just run along and bring us back something to drink. Looks like the place is dry."

"All right, mister. You asked for it," and with that, she storms out of the room ready to make good on her threat.

"Those were the days, I tell you. Things were so much easier. Don't you remember, Sam, when things were easy? We used to go dancing every night."

"I remember," Andrea says, gazing over at him with a fragile look. "I liked it back then. I miss it too."

"I wish they'd put a player in here, Sam. I've told them for years. That's the only way to get the pretty girls to come. All the pretty girls like to dance," he says, giving her a gentle pat on the face with his delicate, glossy hands. "You'll tell 'em for me, won't you, Sam? Me and you, we'll get a new player in here."

And Andrea nods and mutters, "Yes, I'll tell them, as soon as I can," and they go back to playing their game or whatever they're doing with those cards.

Looking at the three of them over there, it's as though I'm getting lost in some movie from the 40s or something, one of those old black and white pictures with all the pretty women who used to dress up in those long, flowing gowns. I look over at the two of them, Andrea and that strange man who feels so familiar, and expect them to any minute get up and start prancing around the room in their dancing costumes.

Then Allison trudges through the door with two young guards in tow, one of them holding some type of baton between his two hands, like he's ready to crack that guy's skull open if he causes any trouble.

"Hey buddy. That's enough. It's time to go," the guard on the right says, at first keeping his distance.

But the man just sits with his back against them, covering his cards like he's trying to hide a winning hand.

"Hey Randle, is that you? I can't be leaving now. I think I'm getting lucky for a change. You wouldn't mind holding up for me, would ya?"

"Hey buddy, we've got to go. Put the cards down and walk over to the door before there's any trouble."

"Randle always was an old stick in the mud. Always knew how to ruin a good hand. Well Sam," he says, looking over at Andrea, "I think I might have to take my ride before I get left behind. It sure is sad to have to leave so early." And then he gets up from his chair and pats down on his pockets to make sure he hasn't forgotten anything. "You'll remember about that player, won't you? You need to start dancing again."

And she leans over and takes his hand and quietly whispers, "I won't forget. I promise."

"That Sam always was a good girl," he says, wagging his head and making his way over to the guards. "Well boys, I guess it's time to go," he tells them as if they're casually giving him a lift back home. "I sure will miss this old place." And with that, he starts making his leave towards the door, with the two guards surrounding him. Then he pauses.

"Hey, I don't remember seeing you," he says, looking straight over at me, with eyes wide open, like he's trying to figure something out. "No, you don't belong here."

And he starts to walk over.

"What are you doing? This place isn't for you."

"Okay, buddy," says the guard, walking up behind him. "It's time to go. I'm not going to ask so nicely again."

"No, I don't have to go. She does. She doesn't belong here. This place isn't for her." And he reaches over to grab me, his long, jagged fingernails scratching the surface of my right arm.

"Let's go," the guard says, this time putting his heavy, muscular arms around the man's delicate shoulder as if telling him it's gonna get rough if you don't step back and come with me immediately.

"No, she needs to leave. I belong here."

"Okay buddy, it's time to go," and the second guard comes to grab him by the other shoulder.

But he stares right into my brown eyes as if he's seeing something inside my subconscious that I didn't know was there. I can feel his hands reaching through me, trying to pull it out.

"I was on a plane. Two planes. One flew east. One flew west."

He struggles to come towards me. The men start pulling him in the other direction. "You don't belong here," he repeats.

"But I do. I was born dead. I never had a chance."

They've got him in a stronghold and begin to drag him away, with his arms held behind his back.

But he screams and moans as if recalling a painful memory, ranting like a madman lost in the agony of his own mind. If there were a magnifying glass waving over my soul, it would look like the sound of that sorrowful voice.

"They just took me. There was ocean and fire falling from the sky."

The guards continue to pull him away.

I just watch.

Then he breaks free, rushing over to tell me something as if knowing he only has a moment to do so. "I was born dead. But you can get out."

And with that, the guards come over and knock him on the head with that baton.

"Just calm down, girls," the burly one says as he starts turning into the hallway with the man's comatose body hanging in his arms. "He wouldn't have hurt you. He was just lost."

And then they were gone.

"Fucking place," Allison says. "They let those loonies walk around wherever they want, and we're the ones locked up in here."

The skin on my eleven-year-old legs sticks to the warm vinyl seat of the school bus, scraping up and down on the ripped cushion from the bumpiness of the bus. There is a hard grating sound. It stops, and three junior high kids get off. I watch them, two boys and a girl, smile and laugh. They are happy. They will do something fun now that school is over. The next stop is my own; but I will not laugh with the boys who get off the bus. And we will not do something fun now that school is over. They will chase me back to my house, and if I can outrun them, I will go home and cry. Tomorrow morning, the day will start again.

Six

It's 8:30 now, and I finally make it into breakfast, about an hour late. Everybody has already left, probably already huddling in the rec room waiting for that old Holocaust survivor. Dana said, "Girls, please be ready at 8:30 prompt. We don't want to be rude. When Gerda arrives, we should all be ready, waiting for her." But I know her gig. She's always about a half hour off, always telling the rest of us to make sure we're there at 2:00 when she doesn't have any plans to start our meetings until 2:15 or 2:30.

There are only two other girls, who I don't recognize, left in the cafeteria. They are part of another group and may have just arrived a day or so ago. I wonder what their stories are. They sit, tucked away in the back corners, trying not to be noticed, staring at their plastic trays of cafeteria food, swirling around overly cooked oatmeal or mushy eggs that look like they've been dosed with yellow food coloring. I nonchalantly walk over to the counter where I hope I can still convince Gloria to serve me breakfast even though I can see she is already cleaning up. Offering a casual smile, I look to the girls and offhandedly scan their bodies to see if there are any markings that might clue me in on their reasons for being here. So far, I can't tell. I've never been good at being sly or secretive, and I'm afraid I'll make them feel self-conscious if I stare for very long.

"Lisa, you're late again. All I have left is oatmeal, which I know you don't like," Gloria says, trying to be stern with me. But I have gotten to know her too well. I know she would pull out everything she had in that old refrigerator to make me some gourmet breakfast rather than see me go hungry. Gloria is a heavyset woman who believes in Jesus and is constantly talking about her seven grandchildren. She says I remind her of one of them. Casey, I think her name is. She also has brown eyes, she tells me. Gloria says Casey likes to write poems, just like me. She always hollers at me across the cafeteria when everyone has left, and I'm still there nursing my food and trying to finish a poem or something I started in the night. "How's the writing going today?" she'll usually ask, but I just look up and smile in a way that keeps her from asking too many questions.

"Whatever, I'm good with the oatmeal today," I tell her. And she says, "Well, Lisa, you should've gotten here an hour ago with the rest of the crowd if you wanted anything else," as she is chopping up fresh fruit and looking into the refrigerator to see what else she can pull out for me. This Gloria, she's a nice woman, maybe one of the nicest I've ever met. Sometimes when I pray I ask God to help her lose weight because she is so fat I'm afraid that one day she will just collapse over that stove when she is here early in the morning cooking us breakfast.

I'm just about to dig my fork into the hard-boiled eggs that Gloria found left over in the fridge, when I hear the sound of high heels quickly tapping down the hallway. I know immediately that my breakfast is over. There's only one person who insists on overdressing for this run-down old house. "Lisa, what are you doing? Gerda's about to walk into the rec room. Come on, let's go," Dana says and waits, staring at me, till I get up to follow her.

Dana is more overdressed than usual. She has on a formal brown suit and a shirt that's buttoned up tightly to her neck. She sees Gerda walking down the hallway and drags me over, holding onto my wrist.

"Hello, Gerda. I'm Dana. We spoke on the phone yesterday," she says politely, reaching out to carefully shake Gerda's hand as if it's made out of something fragile enough to break. "This is Lisa. I think you two have some things in common. She is also a writer," she says, making my face turn red. Gerda is a tender woman who reaches over to rub her hand behind my back, the way my grandmother would if I did something she was proud of. Gerda is also very old. There are tunnels of wisdom ingrained throughout her face. That is my first impression. Wisdom. Or maybe it was too many years of misery.

"Oh, that's wonderful, Lisa. I don't know if Dana told you,

but I'm a writer too. What do you like to write about?"

For some reason, I freeze up and don't know what to say, so I just smile, hoping someone will continue with the conversation without noticing that I am too shy to answer. I look to Dana like a little girl who stares into her mother's eyes for protection. Gerda can tell, at the moment, words are too difficult for me, so she continues to tell me about herself. "I like to write poetry," she tells me, giving me a soft wink with her left eye. "I also wrote an autobiography of my experiences during the war."

"I like to write poetry too," I finally force myself to tell her, though I'm not sure why I am so embarrassed to speak with her. Then she asks if I will share some of my writing with her, and I say yes. And just as I'm about to open my mouth to tell Gerda about a poem I wrote the other night about the mockingbirds that live in the yard in the back of my parents' house, Dana hurries us into the rec room.

"Well, we should go and get started," she says, pushing me towards the door. "I'm sure Gerda would like to talk to you about your poetry afterwards." And Gerda just smiles at me and says of course.

They enjoy the power high school gives to their fourteen-year-old lives. Blonde hair, blue eyes, and deep matching dimples on the lower parts of both of his cheeks, Josh is the picture of the perfect ninth grade boy. Paul is tall and skinny and has a slight acne-tainted complexion. They push themselves higher as cool, tough, popular guys as they push me down. I sit in front of them in homeroom. There are only three minutes before the bell. I can hear their voices in my head already. They throw insulting notes in paper dripping with saliva in front of my face. I sit there, scared, nervous, sweating. Homeroom is ten minutes long. There is nothing for the teacher to do. He sits, quietly, and grades papers, ignoring the class in front of him. In the back of the room, others watch as Josh and Paul try to get my attention. Their insults and stupid jokes get louder and heavier. They make others around them laugh. I can feel the September heat swell in my body; it makes my breathing quick and my stomach sick.

Dana

"Lisa, you keep staring at me all morning like there's something you want to say. Is there something you want to say, to me and to the rest of the girls?"

Oh fuck. We're already an hour and fifteen minutes into this stupid group session, and I thought maybe I would actually get a break this morning. Andrea's been crying about her stupid mother for the past hour, and I thought by the way that was going, it could last all morning and all afternoon. Now what am I supposed to do, put my two cents in about this futile conversation? Andrea's mother was a drunk. My mother wasn't a drunk. I don't know what I'm supposed to be saying right now, but if I don't say some stupid shit, Dana's gonna go on and on until I do. All right. Here I go. "Well, to be honest Dana, I just think you're wrong."

"Okay, Lisa. I'm listening. What do you think I'm wrong about?"

"Well, for starters, I don't think Andrea needs to make up with her mother. I'm not suggesting that she go back to the city to live with Bobby or anything, but I suppose there are other options than just going back to a place where she was miserable. And all I'm hearing out of Andrea is how much her mother drinks, so why the hell would it be a good idea to send someone back to a house where there's drugs and alcohol and fighting all the time. That just doesn't make sense."

"Well Lisa, that is a good point, but right now, her mother is the only family she has since we are unable to find her sister Michele. Don't you think it's important to have contact with your family?"

At eight years old, she knelt on an alter in a white embroidered dress, praying that Jesus would purge her of her sins. With her knees bent and her fingers held tightly at her heart's center, she felt all the transgressions of her young life spin through her mind like a southern storm. Then she spread her mouth open wide so that the old priest could lay a piece of her savior on her eight-year-old tongue. Once she said her amens and let that wafer dissolve on the roof of her mouth, she would be united with Him forever. When it was finally over and the union was secure, she turned to her left and saw her father, grinning and nodding his head in approval; his only daughter had passed through the most important ritual of her young Catholic life, and he was proud. He gave her a smile filled with satisfaction and then the two of them turned to walk down the aisle to the back of the church. When the ceremony was over, and the forty little brides had all taken their vows to be faithful to Jesus, Benedetta and her father went back to the apartment with the rest of their family.

After she made the initial slice in her communion cake with the pink sugary flowers that lined the edges, the newly consecrated girl raised a glass with the rest of her family and tasted champagne for the first time. Then the attention dispersed, and Benedetta's father led her away to his bedroom where the two of them could be alone for the first time since before the service.

"Benedetta," he said. "This is a present from your mamacita up in heaven. She left this for you before she died." And with those

words, Benedetta's father handed her a tiny square box with a light aqua ribbon tied around it, which Benedetta quickly unwrapped, so she could get to the present inside that her mother had left her before she was born.

"Turn around. Let me put it around your neck. Now you can have Jesus and your mamacita with you at all times," he told her as he fastened the clasp for the opal cross that Benedetta's mother had chosen for her when she saw the baby cry in a summer dream one August night before Benedetta was born and knew that she would never live to see the baby's face come out of her body.

"No, Dana, I don't. I don't think it's important to have contact with your family, especially when they have been the source of misery in your life. Maybe it's better just to leave things the way they are and move on."

I can tell all this talk is making Andrea nervous. She's retreating. Her head's starting to fall behind her knees. And those fingertips. Let's just say that they're looking pretty bad. "Really, Lisa, it's okay. I want to make up with my mother, I do. I want to go back to live with her, I do. I think it's the best thing for me," she says, and I just look at her and nod and give her a faint smile, so she thinks that I agree with her. "Sure Andrea, it's the right thing," I tell her with my eyes. I keep everything else that I want to say inside because I don't want to make her feel smaller than she already does. With Andrea, I think it's better just to agree because she doesn't understand the greater picture anyway.

But I can see it in Dana's eyes that I started something and she's not gonna give it up now. Her eyes are shifting back and forth between Andrea and me, but I can tell when they're done shifting, they're gonna land right on me and my big fucking mouth.

And here it fucking comes. "You know, Lisa, you bring up some interesting points. But I think maybe what you want to talk about is not necessarily Andrea and her mother's relationship but your relationship with your mother."

I do have to say in Dana's defense at any rate, she is the

master of all this psychoanalytic bullshit. She can flip the world's bullshit right on your back like she was flipping a quarter for a coin toss. And before you know it, she's got the whole circle of bullshit seekers sizing you up and down and trying to suppose for themselves what deep-seeded issues Lisa has with her mommy.

"Yeah, Lisa, we'd all like to hear this shit," Allison says with the smile of a Cheshire cat.

"All right, Allison. When it's your turn to talk, we'll let you know, and you can pick up the baton, but right now, I think we could all agree that we would like to hear from Lisa."

"Yeah, that's all I was saying, Lisaaahhh. Here, let me help you," Allison says in her oh so obvious obnoxious tenor with her gnarly little eyes that stare at me as she leans over to pick up the baton to hold it out in front of my face as if she was trying to do me a favor. But I know her too well. We've been living side by side for too long now, and I can tell she's itching for some type of recharge. Some type of fuel to her fire that she can only get as she bears witness to someone else's demise.

Whatever. Fine. If you want me to go, I'll go. "Yes, I believe we don't *need* people in our lives, at least not in the sense you're talking about. Everybody here knows I fucking hate my mother, and I'm allowed to hate her if I want to. I'm sixteen years old, and I can decide who I want to see and who I don't want to see. And I don't think I ever have to rationalize that to anyone, do you?"

"Well, Lisa, I do. We're here in therapy, and the point of therapy is to talk about things. To get things off of our chest so that we can heal. I think there's more to the story about why you hold so much resentment towards your mother, and, yes, I think it would be healthier for you to talk about it rather than just to keep it all inside."

"There's nothing to talk about. She's a fucking cunt, and I hate her."

"You know we're not suppose to be talking like that."

You know what. I'm just gonna take a deep breath and go along with it. She's right in a way. I'm getting too angry. I always get too angry. And that's what they want. That's what everybody wants, to see me fall apart. But I'm not gonna give in to them anymore. I just look at her with a straight face and say, "You're right, Dana. It's an inappropriate use of language, and I should be more civil to show respect to you and my peers."

But Dana just looks at me and grins. She's not buying my line of bull. "Right, Lisa. It would be nice to think that you meant any of that, but let's move on. We were talking about your relationship with your mother."

And I agree, sarcastically but with a congenial face, "We were."

"And you were going to tell us why you hold so much resentment towards her."

"You know, we were talking about control, I believe.

Taking control of and having control of one's life. And I've decided I'm going to take control of mine. And the first thing I'm going to do is eliminate the people and places in my life that I hate. And I hate my mother, so she's out."

"Right on, sister. Now you're talking. Elimination is the key to a healthy mind. Throw me a high five, girl," and Allison gestures towards me with her right hand held over her head, and I in return give her a light nod to shut her up.

"All right, Allison. Thanks for the show of support," and Dana faintly rolls her eyes like she usually does when Allison makes some irrelevant comment. She thinks she's doing it subtly so no one can see, but Dana never learned the art of subtly, or at least it doesn't come naturally, so the little eye rolls are apparent to all of us, including Allison. "All right. You keep saying this over and over again about your mother Lisa, but I'm never really hearing any concrete reasons. I'm sure there's some little anecdote inside of you to share, so the rest of us can be enlightened, even a little bit, about why you hate your mother so much."

And I just stop and think for a second if there's any little bullshit story I can throw back in her face just to get her to shut up for five fucking minutes or perhaps throw a curve ball in the direction of one of the other girls, anything to get the heat off me for a change of pace. But suddenly something happens beyond my control; I allow my weakness to take over and blurt out what I don't want anybody to hear. "Because she ignores me," I say in a soft voice. "That's why I hate her." And they all just look at me as if they know exactly what I'm talking about.

Eight

I walk into the rec room sandwiched in between Gerda and Dana and see Sara in the corner of my eye waving at me to come over and sit next to her. I can tell she has saved me a seat. I have to squeeze myself between all the others who probably got there bright and early and have been waiting patiently for the past half hour. I feel like one of those kids who cuts into a long line at an amusement park. I want to stay in the back, but Sara's relentless. She's waving at me with her right hand motioning over her head, and I know there's no way out of going up to meet her.

Almost immediately, Dana walks to the front and gives us a little narrative on Gerda and reminds us all about the Holocaust like we have never taken a world history class. Dana, she always has to make sure she is being thorough, but I think she accidentally takes it too far and sometimes talks to the rest of us like we are ignorant children who haven't experienced enough of the world to know what's really going on. "Girls, Gerda is a Jewish woman who grew up in Germany before World War II. Many of you know that during the war, the Nazis gathered many of the Jewish people in Europe into concentration camps, and many of them died there. Gerda was one of the lucky ones who survived, but many of the people in her family did not. After the war was over, Gerda reunited with her aunt and uncle and relocated to the United States. She has lived here for over sixty years. She would now like to talk to you about some of the experiences she has had in her life."

And Dana walks over to Gerda and shakes her hand and Gerda exchanges her place at the front of the room. Everyone sits quietly and listens as if they all have some type of natural reverence for that old woman. And she deserves it. I can see it all around her face. She is a gentle old woman who has experienced too much grief and suffering to have earned that warm smile she has somehow retained throughout her life. She wears a gold star around her neck like Dana wears her cross. I have seen other people wear similar ornaments, but I'm not exactly sure what they represent. I don't know that much about the Jewish religion, but I've often wondered why so many people hated them so much that they could stand aside and let all of them be murdered like they were.

"It was midnight," Gerda said, "when I was woken up in my bed by the Nazi soldiers. I was disoriented. I didn't know what was going on. There was a pounding at the door, my father answered, and then all of a sudden there were soldiers in my house, coming into my room where me and my sisters were asleep. We all woke up afraid and huddled together in the corner while the men looked though everything in our rooms, I'll never know what for. They acted like we were hiding something, but there wasn't anything in our house to hide. We were just innocent people trying to live our lives. The Nazis said the Jews were evil. They were dirty people who stole money and wanted to contaminate the blood of pure Germans. I was a child. None of that made sense to me. But when the soldiers came into our apartment, all the rumors and all the gossip that surrounded the Jewish ghetto at the time became real to me. And I knew horror in the real sense of the word.

"After they tore apart all the valuables in our small apartment, including the only little doll I had at the time, they just walked out the door with a warning to my father I could not overhear. It's strange to see your father afraid like that. Before, I thought of my father like a Superman, a man of steel who could not be torn apart. But I saw him for the first time for what he really was that night. Just a person, vulnerable and real and afraid that he did not have the power to protect the people he loved in this world. And I knew by looking into my father's eyes that we were in trouble. That the soldiers would be back, and I didn't know what else. I tried to block it out and forget and go on with my daily life like nothing had happened and nothing would happen. But no matter how much you try to hide, I learned, reality will come rushing towards you with all the force and all the stamina of a restless tornado."

It was hypnotizing listening to Gerda. Her demeanor was so comforting. Something inside wanted to run up and crawl into her arms like she was my grandmother sitting on her worn out polyester couch. Instead, I kept thinking of my own father, and what I did to him. That night at the hospital was the first time I really saw who *my* father was.

I was so out of it. I didn't know what was going on. They had me on something strong. For some reason, they wouldn't let both of my parents in to see me at the same time. And when my father came, he was crying so hard. He could hardly speak. He just kept saying, "Lisa, why did you do this? Why would you want to hurt yourself like this?" and I couldn't think of anything to say but, "I'm sorry, I'm sorry." A part of me really was. I was sorry for hurting him. I was sorry for taking his daughter away, like I didn't even belong to myself. I wasn't even thinking of what I wanted, only of what I was taking away from him. How could I think of anything else with the way he was looking at me, the way he was crying? After, I just fell asleep. I woke up with Dana and a nurse sitting by my bed.

"When you were at that camp, you never thought about dying? You never thought that it might be easier that way?" That's Samantha. I only met her once during some group activity. She had burn marks all over her body. I didn't ask her about them, but Allison later told me that her father set their house on fire when she was only seven, and Samantha, her mother, and her sister were all still inside, sleeping. That's what Allison said, anyway. But, you know, she's kind of full of shit, so I never know what to believe when it comes out of her mouth.

"You know, honey, I did every day. There never was a day that went by that I didn't think about it. There never was a time when I didn't see a rope or a knife, a piece of glass even, and didn't think about all the things I could do with something like that if I picked it up in my hand. I don't really know what stopped me. Maybe it was a higher power. Maybe it was just human instinct to survive. But every time a thought like that came into my head, I somehow had the courage to push it away. Something inside of me knew it was worth it to go on."

Worth it to go on. Why, I kept thinking, why would it be worth it? I was hypnotized by that thought, thinking of all the things that could possibly be worth it and whether there might be anything ahead of me that could possibly make me happy. And I guess I must have been mumbling to myself because before I knew it, I was saying it out loud. "Why?" I said, though I didn't really mean to, and as soon as it happened, heat wrapped itself around my skin like a snake choking me. It was hard for me even to look at Gerda in the face.

"That's a good question, Lisa. It would have been hard for me to grasp the horrors that are capable of erupting in the human soul before any of that happened. I just couldn't believe, every day, that all of that was really happening. I almost convinced myself that it was a nightmare, and that somehow I would just wake up from it all. But I went on, Lisa, and I'm glad that I did. There were better times ahead of me, and I'm happy that I stuck around to see them, even if I had to go through all that horror to get to them."

And even though Gerda was speaking to me, I just couldn't help but look over at Andrea, in the corner of the room, sucking on her fingers like a little child sucking on a pacifier. I know Andrea. She is too shy to say anything, but I could tell she wanted Gerda to keep talking. She wanted to believe in the hope she was talking about; she was almost salivating over those ideas, that there could be happy times ahead of her. I think deep inside Andrea, there is, and there always has been, some idealized world of a happy life, of a good husband, of a close family, a safe little house she could live in where she wouldn't be tormented by so many things around her that said, "No, no, no, you're not worth it."

Her mother wanted her to have long, flowing blonde hair that she would wear loosely down her back, except, of course, when she was dancing, and then she could spin it around and around into a beautifully spun heavy bun gently held to the top of her head. Ballet dancers always have long, beautiful hair, so that's what Andrea's hair would look like.

Before the heavy times of her mother's drinking, Andrea's mind goes back and back and listens to the sound of old music waving up and down with the bumpiness of a vinyl record player. There are no words, but the music is soft and the instruments flow into each other. She can see herself at four years old, lightly spinning, listening to the instruments, and her body flowing to the rhythm. Her eyes are closed, and she smiles as she turns around and around with bare feet and a knee-length flowered skirt over the brown carpet of her living room. She can hear Michele. She is laughing; she says, "Look, Mama, look at me spin."

"Oh, look how beautiful. My two ballerinas."

When Andrea opens her eyes, she sees two hands reaching out in front of her. She lifts her hands up and takes a hold of them. Her mother bends her hips down slightly and then bounces her legs back up again; her arms flow loosely with Andrea's as she teaches her daughter to move in the same way. Together, they bend their legs up and down to the music as they slowly spin in small circles and make a larger path around the room. Slow and rhythmically, Andrea follows her mother's feet and the waving of her arms and can feel the tender cadence of the music with the violins that sound smooth and light. She can feel her smile and her four-year-old happiness as she looks up to her mother's gentle face and listens to the easy joy of the record player. They are light and graceful together, and Andrea holds her mother's hands tightly in her own. She won't let them go. They are hers forever.

Nine

"Okay, girls. Seven. Eight. Nine. We're missing one. Does anyone know where Allison is? Yes, Andrea?"

"She's with the doctor. I know she had an appointment this morning. I don't think she's coming."

"All righty then. Let's go ahead and proceed. Everybody. Cross legs. Back straight. Eyes closed. I'm going to tap the bell three times. Then we'll start with a long, deep breath in. Hold. Then push it all out. As we do this, count your breath. One, two in. Hold. One, two, out. As we repeat, try to increase the numbers. One, two, three. Hold. One, two, three out. Remember, as we breathe in, we try to empty our minds and visualize a color. Today we will use orange. When we breathe out, we release."

That's Carol, our yoga teacher. We take yoga two days a week. Tuesday and Thursday mornings at 8:00 am sharp. It's an optional activity, which means we're not forced to come. I guess we could sleep in an extra hour or go to breakfast early or some shit, but I like it here. I like yoga. For most of the time, we just sit with our eyes closed and think about colors. This breathing and these colors, it's supposed to make us clear our minds, so we can fall into a meditation or some shit, but it's not so easy to do. I close my eyes and try to be quiet, but all I hear are thoughts ricocheting through my mind. I want to stop them, but they are always there, even through all this breathing.

I hear Amanda and Andrea talking in front of me.

"Why isn't Allison here?"

"She had a doctor's appointment."

"With Dana?"

"No, with the other doctor from the hospital. Dr. Zen something-or-other. You know, the one she doesn't like."

"The one that electrocutes her?"

"Yes, that one."

"Was she doing something bad again?"

"I don't know. I think she just has to go once a week now. I heard Dana talking about it the other day."

"Girls, shhhh. Just breathe. Quietly. Eyes closed," Carol warns. We are not allowed to talk during yoga. She's actually pretty strict about it. I've seen her kick quite a number of people out of these classes for doing the same thing. Allison, surprisingly enough, several times. I'm surprised she's being so lenient on Amanda and Andrea today. I think she likes Andrea because she used to be a dancer, and she can bend her body into better positions than any of the rest of us.

"Okay girls. Breathe in. Breathe out. One more time. The third time you hear the bell ring, we will open our eyes, slowly."

Now we stand up and do sun salutations for about ten minutes. I like this too, I suppose.

"Okay. Up with our arms over our heads as high as we can reach. Touch the ceiling. Arch back. Then fall forward to your feet."

"They caught her stealing meds. That's why she's not here. They found them when they checked her room the other day." That's Ashley. She's like Amanda. They put a tube into her stomach to force her to eat. I saw it once. It was hard to look at.

"She was high as a kite yesterday at breakfast. She threw a whole glass of orange juice right at that nurse, Jackie. Got juice all in her eyes and everything. That's why they sent her next door." That's Sienna. Her room is down the hall. I don't know what her story is.

"I didn't hear no bullshit story like that. If that happened, I would have heard."

"Yeah, well, I *did* hear."

"From who?"

"From a source."

"Yeah. Whatever."

"Well, you didn't see her all day yesterday, did you? You just look tonight. I bet Jackie comes in with a cut next to her left eye, just like Kellie told me."

"Kellie. Well that explains a lot."

"Girls, I'm hearing chattering again. What do I have to do? Okay. Everybody. Quiet. Stand straight. Eyes closed. Hands at heart's center. Deep breathing. In. Out. In. Out. Until you hear the bell."

I wonder what she got herself into this time.

"Okay. Eyes open. Let's go back to the floor. Right leg straight. Left leg bent and placed over the right. Then turn to the left with our right elbow over our left knee. And hold."

"What do you mean electrocuted?" I ask Andrea as I bend over to the left.

"They're shocking her once a week because she's crazy, and she takes too many drugs. They only do that to the really bad ones."

"No, they don't do that anymore. That's just an old wives' tale."

"A what?"

"You know, an old wives' tale," but she just looks over with an absent stare. "You know, a bullshit story, a rumor, something that isn't true."

"Oh no, Lisa, it's true. My old neighbor, Karen. You know the girl that used to room next to me," she clarifies. "She was really out there. They brought her in from the streets, just like Allison. And she got the same thing. Every week. Until she just lost it forever. And they had to lock her away in the crazy ward next door. They took her out of here screaming and yelling and breaking things. They even put her in a straightjacket. That's the first time I ever saw somebody in one of those things."

"No, when was this?"

"A few months ago. It was before you got here. Honest. Ask Amanda. It all happened right in front of me. Pinky swear," and she gets herself out of that pose she's in to hold that pinky finger of hers right in front of my face. "Honest, Lisa, I swear."

"I believe you, Andrea. You can put your finger down."

"Okay, ladies. Up on your feet. Tree Position."

Oh, I like this one. We have to balance on one leg. For some reason, I'm pretty good at it. I can stay up for the full three minutes, usually more than anyone else. I always see them with their legs sliding down or falling over to the floor, and I just stand there as straight as an arrow with my hands in the air, high above my head. If Dana could see me, I'm sure she'd read into it with some psychiatric bullshit. I'm glad she kind of stays out of this class.

Every sound bounces through my mind like the loud, hard pounding of a metal ball trapped within the barrier of a pinball machine. I start to walk slowly, spacing out the time when I will be locked in front of my morning English classroom, unsympathetic eyes staring in my direction, my mind cramped and crippled from forty-eight hours without sleep. I am first today to give my presentation on the role of women in One Flew Over the Cuckoo's Nest. Josh and Paul will be sitting in the front row. My legs hold me up, but my mind is black and wavy, my stomach is nauseous, my body is hot. It is 8:53. My feet begin to slow down their steps.

Amanda

She's on a roll this morning, and the two of them are gonna have a go at it, I know it. Dana likes to pretend she can suck it all up and retain this calm composure, no matter what shit's been slung in her direction. But Allison's got a rare face on. There's a heightened peak to her obnoxious posture that's filling the air like freshly baked bread coming out of a bakery oven. We've been sitting here, trying to have a discussion on why Amanda has been refusing to eat for the past three days, and every time Dana gets Amanda to utter some small phrase, which by no means is an easy task, Allison just blows in full steam ahead with some unrelated comment that's making us all wish the arrow on the clock was a little closer to 11:30 am, so we could all get the fuck out of here as soon as possible.

"Well, everybody knows that blondes have more fun."

"Yes, Allison, is there some point you're trying to make?" Dana asks, struggling to maintain her tranquility even though I can tell she is starting to unravel. Allison won't stop playing with those dried out, bushy dreadlocks of hers, and every time she tries to twirl one around her fingers, white, flaky debris drips out of her hair, shedding like a dehydrated paste that's been sticking to the back of her scalp for years. There's so much of it that it's been piling up on the floor underneath her chair for nearly an hour. I don't think she's even conscious of the unhygienic mess she is creating, but I can't keep my eyes away from it, and I've been watching Dana's eyes spy her movements since group began this morning at 9:30. "I'm not really sure of the connection you're trying to make here Allison between Amanda's problems and the color of her hair," implying with the movement of her eyes that she didn't need Allison to elaborate in order for the meeting to proceed.

"I'm just trying to point out that sometimes even little subtle changes can make a big difference in our lives. Look at me. Several years ago, I decided to make some changes to my hairstyle, and I began to feel more comfortable with myself. Amanda has beautiful dark colored hair, but perhaps she could feel a little bit different inside if she made some drastic changes to it. I mean, come on Amanda, not that I'm encouraging promiscuity or anything, but you're sixteen years old. What the fuck are you waiting for? You need to get out there and start exploring what Mother Nature intended for you to explore, and then maybe you'll feel a little better about yourself and food won't be your own worst enemy."

"Sixteen's not that old, Allison. I don't think you should be encouraging Amanda to go out there and start engaging in sexual relationships before she's ready. Perhaps that's something you should think about as well. Perhaps you were too young to handle being in so many of those relationships yourself. Perhaps you could handle your private emotions better if you took more time to self-reflect on your own feelings and not be so often engaged in relationships with other people, specifically older men."

"Well, Dana. I'm sixteen, and I think I'm old enough to be in sexual relationships if I want to be. We're too sexually inhibited in this country. If we all learned to relax a little more, maybe everyone wouldn't be walking around with such a pole up their ass all the time."

And I can tell Dana's fuming. She's so vigorously tapping that pen against her notebook that little pieces of plastic are about to explode and blue ink's gonna start gushing out everywhere, staining all the rugs and all the furniture she tries so hard to keep neat and organized. Dana. You know, even though Allison is the queen bee of any pain-in-the-ass I have ever met, I have to admit, something, that I'm holding down deep inside, is getting my juices flowing just about now, watching that straight face Dana tries so hard to maintain struggle to keep those fine lines around her eyes from bunching up.

"First of all, Allison," Dana says with the tap of her pen

getting stronger and more emphatic, "we've had the discussion too many times about the language that's appropriate in this group. Second of all, I don't think the solution to the great problem of American society is for everyone to become more sexually free, as you would call it. And finally, I do very much appreciate any help you can add to the conversation we began this morning on *Amanda's* problems and *Amanda's* life, but if you don't have some specific, mature comment that you can add to the conversation we were having about Amanda's eating habits, then perhaps you should wait until it is your turn. I don't think I have to remind you that you are not holding the baton at the moment."

"What-evvverrr. I'll just sit here and look pretty."

And Dana takes a deep breath to reposition her Zen and, with a quick and extremely obvious roll of the eye, casually lays her left hand over her right to stop her overzealous ticking and turns her attention back to Amanda. "Okay, Amanda, why do you think it's so difficult for you to put food into your mouth?"

"I don't know. I just hate the way it feels when it's inside my body. It's just makes everything in me feel tense and bloated. I just feel so disgusted with myself after I eat," she says in a shallow voice with eyes looking down to the floor and feet circling the carpet in front of her.

"Do you remember a time when you had a better relationship with food? When it was a little easier for you to eat?"

"I guess I didn't mind eating so much when I was a little

kid. But it was different then. I could eat anything I wanted and still be as skinny as a rail."

"So, that's an interesting point. It's not necessarily the food, but it's the weight that you find problematic?"

"Yes, I hate the way it makes me feel so heavy. I hate the way I look after I've eaten."

When Amanda was twelve, in the summer before eighth grade, she went swimming in a shaded creek of dirty water and a thirsty parasite swam through the pores in the bottom of her feet and brought sadness throughout her entire body. It didn't make a permanent home. From time to time, it would leave like a vapor, transcending her physical body and moving back into the air where it originally came from. But then she would wake up from a long sleep at the end of a cold winter and before she knew how to put up her defenses, the sadness was back again.

And so it was, from then at twelve, until now at sixteen, that sadness would come and go as it pleased, moving through her unwelcoming skin like a snake slithering in and out of a land it did not belong to until Amanda decided to cut the blood from outside her body and kill the snake forever.

Years of life with motley feelings of reds and blues and greens and yellows stitched the quilt of those unwelcomed years when she was moving through a new period she was supposed to enjoy. Adolescence should be springtime with new flowers of soft colors, her mother thought, but the April rains that bring life to those colors stayed for too long in Amanda, and every year, before she knew it, fall would be coming again, and life would be crusted over, dark and brown and ready to break, and then Amanda, exhausted from all the rain and all the falling, would lay her head down on the early winter snow, and stay there, silent and sleeping, until the rains came again in April.

This is how her mother learned grief, for all she wanted since the first time she felt Amanda move was to watch her daughter laugh and smile, knowing that there was a fire and glow inside of her. But the pilot light of Amanda's life blew out from a cold winter's storm, and all the love and all the smiles from Amanda's mom and Amanda's dad, her grandmother and her cousins, all the voices of love all around her, were not enough to relight the flame, so darkness grew inside of her, stitching itself up tight through all the seasons of her life for four long years, holding her so close to the ground that she simply forgot that the earth ever moved, that the weather ever got warmer or the sun ever came out.

But every once in a while, when the clouds began to break and the blue became visible, Amanda's eyes would bring her smile back into herself and chase the sadness away, and at the end of a wavy path, she would always wind up at the same place--her mother's face. That was the only safety she ever knew and that was the only picture she would remember and take back with her when the sadness came again, and she was forced to look through the distorted lens of blackness. Her mother, with thin, silky, soft colored brown hair that fell between her shoulders, toasted almond colored eyes that blended in with her bangs, and lightly shaded pink lips, the color of strawberries at their peak, who smiled with such concern at her only child in the morning when she would wake her and in the evening when she lay with her in bed, desperately trying to free Amanda from a darkness she did not understand.

But her mother learned through a wicked, evil darkness of her own, that a human's mind and a human's body cannot endure constant grief over the person who she loves the most, so all this sadness and all this grieving settled in the skin of her own body and grew in a different form, a heavy, brown spot that grew like a seed in the bottom left side of her young breast. And it grew and grew on the inside until she could feel it on the outside, and the doctor told her it was too late—the darkness would not leave—it would stay there forever, sucking and sucking all the life out of Amanda's mother, down inside of itself, the tumor growing stronger and darker, as the young woman fell smaller and weaker, and the young girl watched as her only brightness melted into nothing and died on top of a yellow hospital bed, leaving the sadness inside of Amanda forever.

Without the light of her mother's eyes to bring her back into the soft periods of relief in her own life, Amanda gave into the sadness, letting it take hold of her, so that the bitter, silent winter was all she felt for half a year until she saw a shining light leaning out of a jar in the kitchen, moving and glowing from the reflection of the roof's skylight. She remembered a light like that once when she was four, and she was skating on a pond with her mom and dad, her hands tight between the both of theirs. She hears their voices now, "Okay, one, two, three, jump," as they lift her gently into the air, and the air makes her giggle. The sky is bright like a spotlight, and the sides of the pond are covered with new snow that sparkles with the moon. That's what she remembers now, light from the moon that made the snow sparkle and the giggles of a four-year-old girl, white light reflecting from the sky, the background smooth and clear, glitter in the air and on the ground.

That's what brought her to that light she saw again in the kitchen, light that came from the corner of the counter that was moving from the reflection of the sun, and she walked and walked until she got close and picked up that knife in her right hand with its maroon wooden handle and slid it like a silky brush over a blank canvass through the upper lines of both of her wrists.

"Ok. Amanda you've been at the house for several months and have been eating a semi-normal diet. How do you feel about yourself now?"

"Well, honestly," she says, still looking towards the floor, "I'm not happy. I feel awful. I feel bloated, and I feel fat, and to be honest, I just want to get out of here so badly so I can go back to feeding myself. I hate having somebody watch everything I eat. I'm not a child," Amanda screams, raising her voice to the point where even people in the hallway stop to look. I think it takes all of us a few minutes to adjust. I don't think I've ever seen Amanda get worked up about anything. "I should be able to make those decisions for myself. I feel like everything I do here is being watched, and I hate it. I just want to go back to being alone the way I was before."

"I hear ya, sister. It's like we're living in *1984* and Big Brother's watching every move we make."

"Really, Allison, is that how you feel?"

"Yeah, as a matter of fact, if you're asking me."

"Well, I wasn't really, but I guess you decided you needed to once again jump in on this conversation without the baton in your hand. And I suppose you feel like it's fair to the other people in this group right now who wait patiently for their turns." And I can see now she's really got Dana's goat. I don't know why it makes me so happy. Something inside is feeling a tad bit sadistic at the moment, but you gotta take it when you can get it, and I can't help but think both Allison and Dana have had it coming in their directions for quite some time now.

"Well, to be honest, that's another thing. Why does everything I say have to be monitored in some type of time apparatus? When I want to say something, I want to say something and not feel like I'm suffocating and you're the noose that's being tied around my neck."

"Well that is some analogy, Allison. We're trying to have civil conversations in this group, and I don't think it's acting that civil towards your peers when you just blurt out anything you're feeling at any time you're feeling it. In life, it's quite appropriate for people to take turns and to respect others when it's their turn and not yours."

"Well I don't really think that's the way real life is at all. When a thought comes to your head, I think it's completely appropriate for you to explore it."

And again I'm watching Dana sit there and suck down her breath as if she's in the middle of some expensive meditation class. She's not used to people talking back, and she's using that breath of hers to buy time so she can mind her way through those ten years of Ivy League schooling she's got underneath her belt. "Okay, Allison, what do you think is the appropriate next step we should take in this meeting? Do you really think it's fair to Amanda what you're doing right now, stealing her time when it's her turn to talk?"

"Stealing her time, that's what I'm doing?"

"Well, do you have a better word for it?"

And Amanda just looks over at the two of them with hurried eyes, trying desperately not to get in the middle of this little duel Dana and Allison have got going on between them. "Really, Dana, I'm okay for the day. I think I would be happy giving Allison the baton," and she reaches over with her hand shaking to give it over to Allison; but Dana intercepts and holds the baton in Amanda's hand tightly with her right fist.

"Amanda, thank you, but I don't think that's the right thing to do."

"The right thing to do?" Allison laughs. "Somebody's mommy was awfully stern with her when she was a baby, wasn't she?"

And that's the bull's eye Allison was aiming for all morning. Dana looks over at her with a look in her eye I've never seen. "Allison, what gives you the right to speak to me, or anybody else for that matter, with that type of tone? Are you the recipient of some type of PhD in psychology that I'm unaware of?" And I can see that something has shaken Dana out of her neatly organized Jell-O mold, and the layers of conformity, that she carefully wraps herself inside of every day as she gets up at 6:00 am sharp, are starting to unravel in a way that Dana's never experienced.

"I don't think I need to have a fancy PhD in psychology to

know that people should be able to talk when they feel like it?"

"People should *not* be able to talk when they feel like it." Dana's like a steam whistle at 4:59 pm, and finally she can't hold it any longer. She's got to let it go. All that anger boosts her off her chair and positions her directly onto those cheap polyester high heels she forces her poor, overworked feet into. "That's not the way a civilized society behaves. We take turns, and we show respect for one another and that's not the way you're behaving right now," she exclaims with a finger pointed directly into Allison's face like a parent scolding her disobedient child.

But Allison, unlike Dana, sits back, relaxing with her right leg casually bent over her left, staring Dana in the eye and calling her out. "Oh, yeah, well what are you gonna do about it, Miss Smarty Pants? What does the grand revisionist of this carefully organized micro-civilization have in mind in order to chastise one of the miscreants?" And she looks over at the rest of us like she's come out on top and there's nothing that Dana can do about it, and I look over at Dana and all that puffiness in her face that looks like it's gonna explode like some marshmallow that's been sitting over a fire for too long. And I sit there and brace myself, trying to settle the anticipation that's been growing over the last five minutes during this unexpected morning buzz.

"Well Allison, that's a terrific question," Dana says as she somehow is able to recover her Buddhist-like composure. "But I'm actually not the great leader of this little microcosm of the civilized world as you'd like to call it. Dr. Zelinski is." And Dana takes that plastic pen of hers that she's been whacking against her notebook all morning long, and gently, with great composure, writes a note in her little book. "I'll be sure to schedule a meeting with him later on this afternoon, so the two of you can come up with an appropriate punishment."

I haven't been here long enough to know the significance of Dr. Zelinski and why he seems so threatening, but just the little mentioning of his name is all Allison needs to regain her composure and act like a child who's just been sent to her room.

Seconds after he let the needle slide out of his arm, the voices of the dead children got softer, smooth and easy like the beat of a John Coltrane song. It was like that from the first time. His buddy Ralphie had been shooting for a while and brought back a pouch big enough to share from a weekend leave to Saigon. They sat there, alone, at the edge of camp, passing an empty bottle back and forth between them, two twenty-three-year-olds near the end of their last tour. They had sucked the last drop of whiskey out of the glass bottle minutes ago, but were too inebriated, so they just kept passing it between them until Ralphie flipped the bottle up into his right hand and threw it like a football spiraling over the thirty-yard line. The bottle fell so far out in the distant night, it was hard for the two drunken boys to see where it fell, but they could hear the glass hit the ground and echo over the hard surface.

"Fuck, you got that thing out there," James said to Ralphie.

"Yeah, had a full scholarship to Ohio State. Then I got the bright idea to enlist. There was no way I was gonna let my kids grow up speaking Russian."

"Well, football will still be there when you get home. So will Ohio State."

"Yeah, I suppose next you're gonna tell me so will my football scholarship."

"You never know. They say we're supposed to get a free ride just for being vets. You could go back man, especially with that throw. I know you can." But it was the alcohol talking and even *through his hazy way of thinking, James knew those kinds of dreams were gone for the both of them. For all of them who were stuck in Vietnam. They would leave, but it would never leave them. Over the years since his eighteenth birthday, James had been home two times between three tours, but he had never really been home. Home was just a memory, just a dream of a life lived so long ago, it seemed now like a fantasy he remembered from a childhood book. He had seen his parents, but he really hadn't seen them. He had sat in his mother's kitchen on Thanksgiving, a golden turkey and homemade pie, just as it looked in those storybook pages of his youth. But the kitchen didn't look the same and the flavors didn't smell as sweet and the voices that each took turns giving thanks before the family carved the bird didn't seem to be speaking to the same God that James remembered. It was a strange God now, one that he had stopped thinking about years ago when his troop raided a small village on the Batangan Peninsula, and the American boys burned to death hundreds of Vietnamese children. The villagers wanted time to gather their belongings, but the soldiers burned everything before they had time to leave. He remembers his captain saying, "We need to show them an example, show them we're not fucking around." It was dark and the village had no electricity. There were only soldiers and the voices of children screaming in a language James did not understand.*

"Hey man, you ever do any of this shit?" Ralphie turned around and put a small sandwich baggie with a white crystal

powder into James' right hand, almost like giving him a handshake, assuring him everything was going to be all right.

"No, man. How long have you been doing that?"

"Not long. It will take the edge off at night. Help you sleep."

"Man, you shouldn't get yourself into that shit." *But Ralphie could tell that James really didn't mean it; he wanted to know the power that was in that plastic baggie for himself. Ralphie knew it by the way that James held onto his hand when he leaned over to give him the heroin.*

James let go of Ralphie but kept the baggie for himself, picked it up in his left hand and held it out in front of him, examining it like he was looking under a microscope for a ninth grade lab science project.

"Help me sleep, huh? Haven't done that in a while."

"Got a needle in my pocket already fixed up, Jimmy."

"Man, I don't want to get hooked on that crap."

"You won't get hooked, Jimmy. When you leave, you leave it here. And never look back at anything."

"Yeah, well, I wouldn't mind sleeping for a while."

My mind snaps out of a deep sleep. I am fully awakened, somewhat confused. I watch the bright red light flash 2:25 in the morning from the corner left side of my room. I am choking. I cannot feel the oxygen in my lungs. I remember yoga and start to slow my breathing down. A deep inhale. A long exhale. At 2:24, I was in high school, alone, in front of my locker, staring at the lock; I cannot remember the combination. I stand there in front of it, shaking and afraid. I cry so hard, it pushes me out of my dream. Now, I am awake, vigilante in my bed, consciously breathing long, deep breaths.

I will make myself stay awake. I will write about the great horned owl outside my window. He is there, up in the tree to the right side of the hospital, sitting there behind the leafless branches, staring at me. The steady cadence of his voice plays till the day breaks. "Who, who, who," he sings, so softly and so tenderly it is as if he is speaking my name, Lisa, in gentle syllables. This great horned owl, he is trying to protect me with this voice, keeping me from going back to my dream.

Amanda will wake me soon anyway. She has bad dreams too. They make her scream. She screams really loudly, but she is still sleeping. Her room is right next to mine. I hear her scream, and then the nurses run in. "Amanda, Amanda, wake up," they say. And then Amanda wakes up, and she starts crying. "My mom, my mom, where is my mom?" she always says, even though we all know that her mother has been dead for a long time. Amanda is young. I don't think she is even sixteen. She might be, but a young sixteen. If I didn't know better, I would think she was still in junior high, just by the way that she looks. Her hair is a very light brown, a very soft color. She says she got that from her mother, that her mother also had a very soft color hair.

Sara was fifteen. She was the youngest. She had strawberry colored hair, like ice cream, like my favorite ice cream. Dana says, try to remember happy things, and sometimes I think about ice cream at the beach. I can remember when I was really little eating ice cream at the beach with my sister, April. I remember the sweetness of the sugar buzzing in my head. We used to go swimming in the salt water, and afterwards my mother held us underneath an outside shower in the parking lot to rinse off. It felt like ice cubes being dropped behind my back, getting trapped between my skin and the lining of my bathing suit. When I was really young, I used to scream, "Stop it, Mommy. It hurts. It hurts," so loudly that other people would look over to make sure my mother wasn't doing anything wrong. I think this would embarrass her, but I was too young to think about anything but the cold water.

I don't usually tell Dana these stories though because then she will use it against me. She will say, "Lisa, I told you that there was happiness in your life." Then she'd make me say other things to her, promise that I want to live.

The great horned owls, they come from Florida, in the Everglades where the alligators live. But there are other types of owls that go further up north, like the western screech owls who go all the way up to Alaska. Up north, there are rainbows in the sky. They dance around in the darkness all winter long. People say they're still there in the summer, but you just can't see them. There is too much light. I don't know. I think maybe they go away because there are too many people outside in the summer. They go out, and then the rainbows go away. Up north in Alaska, it is still dark outside, but not for very long.

I won't make my owl stay here. I will send him back to

where he came from. It is too cold up here anyway. There are others like him that come for me. They sing for me when I'm sad. They say, "Lisa, stop crying," in their soft melodies, but I cry anyway. Lots of people cry. I hear Amanda cry every night. She misses her mother, she says. But I think there are other reasons too. I think she cries because she is too skinny or too fat; I forget. But she wants to be prettier, she says. She wants to be pretty like her mother was, she says. I don't know. I never really thought my mother was so pretty. If she were dead, I don't think I would cry about it so much like Amanda does. I don't know if I would miss her.

Andrea cries. She cries all the time. She cries when we have group meetings and it's her turn to talk. She picks up the baton every time. You would think that she wouldn't want to do that so much because she is always crying, and she mumbles so much. It's almost hard to know what she is saying sometimes. She bites off her fingertips too. I like Andrea, but it's really disgusting. It's hard to look at her when those fingers are up by her face. She puts them in her mouth all the time and chews on them. Dana always says, "Stop that, Andrea. Put your fingers on your lap when you talk," and then Andrea puts her fingers on her lap for about two-point-two seconds, and then up they go again right into her mouth. Dana is trying to get her to live too. She lets her cry all the time during our meetings, because, for some reason, she thinks it is good for Andrea. I know this about Dana. She is a young doctor. A part of me likes her, but I would never tell. But a part of me doesn't like her at all. She wants me to make up with my mother. I don't want to. I never want to see my mother again. I would rather die. I don't care about dying anyway. It doesn't scare me. If I die, I will go to heaven and get wings, so I can fly at night like the great horns.

I bet you Sara has wings, pretty like a butterfly. Pretty orange and black wings like the monarchs have. She had a monarch butterfly on her little purse. She got it when she was living in the city. She traded some kid for something. I forget what it was. I like monarch butterflies. They migrate up to Canada right through New Jersey. I see them every spring, and I think, I wish that I could follow them up north, where everything is frozen, and, in the winter, you look up and see rainbows. But I don't think Sara knew anything about monarchs. I pointed to her patch one time and said that's a pretty monarch, but Sara looked confused. She didn't know what I was talking about. To her, they were all just butterflies.

Eleven

"I'm sorry, Lisa. I'm sorry about what happened. I'm sorry I let you down, and I'm sorry you don't trust me. Can you forgive me?"

"Fuck you."

"Excuse me?"

"I don't fucking believe you."

"Well, I'm sorry about that too."

"Rosemary, why do you think Lisa is so angry with you?" Dana interrupted.

Rosemary took a deep breath and then raised her eyes to the ceiling. "Lisa was always mad at me. Since she was a child, she was always mad at me. Always mad at me or somebody else. What am I supposed to do about that? Me, her father, her sister. Everybody had to always worry about Lisa and what we had to do to make her happy. And I didn't worry enough, is that what you are saying? Well, I'm sorry. I really am, Lisa. You think I enjoy watching you so unhappy, when the truth is, I don't. I don't enjoy watching you suffer. You are my child. I did my best. If you say you forgive me, then we could move on."

But Lisa didn't forgive her mother. Instead, she was confused over the content of the speech she just gave. She never heard her mother talk like that. So cold and so sterile. Like she had rehearsed in front of a mirror over and over and over again last night when she was thinking about what she would say to her daughter, who she hadn't seen in almost a month, who the last time she had seen, was lying on the floor of her bathroom next to an empty bottle of her pain medication and a thin puddle of vodka. Now she didn't know what to say; she had to rehearse a response.

"I don't believe you. You even sound like you're full of shit."

Rosemary looked at Dana. "Well, what am I supposed to do with that? You asked me to be calm. I'm being calm. What am I supposed to do now?"

"Well, Rosemary," Dana said. "I think you could start by being honest. I know that you love Lisa, and you care about what happened, but you need to really tell her. I think Lisa can tell that your feelings are coming across a little artificial. I don't think you are doing this on purpose, and I know this must be difficult for you, but you should try to start over again. Look at Lisa and tell her honestly how you feel."

Rosemary looked at the floor and then up again at Lisa. "I'm sorry, Lisa." Her voice was softer this time. "I know you don't believe that I love you, but I do." Rosemary stopped talking and just looked over at her. "If you would have died, Lisa, I don't know what I would have done. I still can't believe this is happening."

Sara

When Sara was six, her father took her from her mother when she wasn't looking. He wasn't supposed to. Two days later they found her in Arizona. Now, she remembers what it was like to be alone in the hot desert, standing on the highway with no shoes, wanting her mother. The wind so dry and hard it choked the air in her throat. Being alone for so long made her hungry; that's all she remembers. Not fear, but heat in her throat and her stomach breaking, sharply. Now, she remembers sound and can hear thunder rumbling in her stomach mixed in with the blurry wind of the desert.

Time wasn't with her. She doesn't remember time, only a policeman coming to take her away, his brown face and young eyes. He didn't know what she was doing there, with no shoes, walking around the hot, empty road and holding her stomach. One minute listening to the hollow sound of the desert, the next minute his face with his arms shaking her, trying to get words to fall out of her mouth, to tell him why a child was standing alone in the desert.

Now, as she sits quietly, she can hear his voice, scared and mumbling and hard. But still she cannot speak to him; even now, she cannot keep her head still, and she cannot make out his face clearly enough. But she wants to. She is trying to look for him in her six-year-old memories, but all she sees is the brown blur and the young eyes.

She was trapped in a place he couldn't wake her out of. The night before, the first night she spent alone, she created a place inside herself so she could escape the wind and all the other voices she didn't want to hear. She remembers trying to hide underneath a blanket made of sand, but it wouldn't cover her ears, so she just stayed quiet and closed herself deeper inside her own mind. One full night in the desert and no cars and no mom and no blanket, just herself. She had to create the quiet.

In the morning, the crackling in her stomach got deeper. Before the policeman, she thought it would just break the rest of her, but it didn't. When she wouldn't talk back, he took her in his car, and she waited with him in the empty cold station with no other sounds but broken static voices coming from the box on his desk. Now, in her room, she can hear other voices, hidden in the distance, maybe from the window that was sitting to the left. Maybe there were other faces too. She tries, but she cannot see them. Then, when she was six, she just sat there in a hard, wooden chair, her bare feet on cold cement, until her mother came the next day and brought her back to California.

Before this, before the rescue, she drove with her father from one desert to the next, from the vacant eastern border of California through the adjacent empty space of Arizona, everything rolling into each other's place, so she didn't realize she was so far from home. She thought he was taking her around the empty town; she didn't realize how much time had gone by, since he took her, when she was playing alone, outside in the back.

She sees Arizona now—all yellow with brown dried out bushes that tumble as fast as the car and heat that hurts her face.

Along their road, there was nothing—no people, no buildings, no gas stations—only her father in the front seat, hot and yellow, driving over the gray that wouldn't end.

She turns her head to the left and sees him now, next to her, with a small bottle in his left hand, wrapped in a damp brown paper bag like she used to take to school for lunch. The closed window pushing his smell to her nose. On her side, the window was down, and the air was heavy. It hit her hard, but she couldn't stand being in the car without the air, alone with him and his smell. He would be mad if she threw up on her clothing since she didn't have any others. She didn't even have shoes. That's how quickly he took her. She sees him looking at her, playing with the radio, trying to confuse her with a familiar sound, so she wouldn't remember she wasn't with her mother, but all that came through was static that kept breaking into a sharp sound and falling down into static again. She felt hypnotized by the emptiness and the endless road. It kept her still and away from fear.

She's looking at her father again, feeling this same stillness, remembering the sound of the wind rush outside. It was quiet, like sleep in an empty room, when he reached over and put his warm hand between her legs, feeling underneath her skirt. She remembers his smile. He looked over and smiled like he was tucking her into bed. She just stared out the window to the road in front of her, feeling the Arizona desert air warm her body, making her sweat like never before.

All she remembers is the sensation of touch, that warm, sweaty feeling of his hands and the hot, immovable desert air. Her quiet, hypnotic thoughts broke too quickly for her to think about an accident as her head hit against the front of the car, and her body twisted in a strange way that she had never felt before, in circles over and over and over. She tried to count them, but it was too quick. All she could do was listen to the other car that went over the bridge with no water underneath.

When they slowed down, she looked over at her father as he snapped the car wheel, and finally the car just zigzagged, no more circles. Then it stopped, and there was quiet again. No sound outside, and her father said nothing. But he looked at her this time, with no voice, and tried to start the car over again. He kept pushing the key with his wrist, but it wouldn't start the car. She remembers the sound. Almost like coughing. On and off, the car would cough. Then he stopped and looked at her. As he turned his head, he hit his feet hard against the floor. Then, he looked back at the road and made the car cough again.

Finally, he put his hands on his knees and turned his eyes to his lap. Then he looked at her again with an absent stare, still with no words, only the quiet in the car and the whisper through the window from the unfriendly desert breeze. He grabbed the bottle, opened the door, and ran. And she watched him out the same window in which she had watched the endless road that seemed to go on through infinite time during that whole morning and that whole day. Now she knew where that road would lead. It was leading to the place where her father would run.

I close my eyes and breathe in deeply and try to imagine a soothing color, like we learned in yoga. But all I see is black. I take a breath and feel my lungs fill up until I can't go any longer. I hold. Then release. The longer I repeat this breathing process, the easier it is to push everything away. In the back of my mind, everything is blank. It is dark and quiet, and I feel a softness inside, like my grandmother pressing her hands against my chest.

I'm almost lost in this darkness, almost to the point where I can imagine my mind releasing and falling to sleep, when I hear, "That bitch. She moved out there the week after he left. I knew she always wanted to sink her teeth into him," coming right up through my window like a tiny piece of wood slithering underneath my skin, causing an infection.

It's that nurse, Jackie. All night long she talks in an elevated voice, ranting and raving about her ex-boyfriend and her bullshit life. Apparently, from this conversation, he's found someone else.

"You're right, Jackie. She was probably after him the whole time you were in college." That's Margot, the other nurse. Every night, I hear her say, "You're right, Jackie, you're right," like she doesn't have the backbone to tell Jackie what she really means, if she means anything at all. Margot's voice is softer and absent of that obnoxious tinge that Jackie's retains. I watch them, from inside my window, talk under the spotlight at the front door. They're both out there smoking like they've just won an endless supply of Camels with some lucky Scratch 'n' Play card from 7-Eleven.

Sometimes I think they can smell the smoke coming from my room, but they don't care because they're always doing things they're not supposed to be doing. The other night, it was one of those nights when I was staring at the ceiling till four in the morning. And I couldn't concentrate on anything with all that jibber-jabbering going on, so I figured I would take a walk in the hall for a bit, seeing as the two people who were supposed to be out there monitoring that hall seemed to be preoccupied with their own bullshit.

With the nurses outside, everything is quiet. I leave my shoes behind and walk out on that cold marble floor, barefoot for the first time. I think about Sara. She must have felt that same cold sensation from the marble floor ringing up through her body that I'm feeling right now. I wonder what gave her the strength to run into the sky like she did. I look and look for it, but I can't seem to find that same strength inside myself. Not this evening anyway.

She remembers the first time she learned about Jesus. She was eight years old and her mother's new boyfriend Angelo was telling her the story of the Nativity. How God sent his only son to save her.

They left California in early February, so Sara had to start the new school in the middle of the year. Her mother met Angelo, the assistant principal, on a March Monday morning, coldness in the air and whistles in the wind unlike either one of them had ever heard. Sara and Veronica, her mother, walked into his office at 9:07 that morning with rosy red cheeks and frozen little fingers that couldn't move.

"My goodness. Here are the lovely ladies from California. My, my, you sure are lovely, but we sure are going to have to get you two some winter coats. We wouldn't want either one of you to come down with something."

By 9:53, Angelo was thanking Vicky for her dinner invitation and assuring her that he would be at their apartment with wine and flowers at seven o'clock sharp on Friday evening. "Can't wait to try your delicious Southern California cooking."

They had to rush out of California. Veronica had forgotten about the time until she was scheduling her next appointment to get her nails done--florescent pink polish with silver rhinestones on the left and right ring fingers, she reminded the woman. "Okay," she said. "January 25. 5:00 pm. We'll see you then."

That's when it hit her. It was January, and her ex-husband would be up for parole next month. Two years and up for parole already for kidnapping their only child. No, now he would never get the chance to see Sara again. She went home. Threw anything she saw as valuable into a few old falling apart suitcases and told Sara they had to leave. By the end of the week. Take only what you need.

"But why, Mommy? Where will we go?"

"It doesn't matter. Far, far, away."

"Why, Mommy? I want to stay in California."

"No, no, we have to go now. Next month, when your father gets out, he won't know where we are. He's too stupid to find us and too lazy to look. No, if we go now, he'll never know where we are, and I'll finally be rid of that man."

She was too beautiful, so she had too many boyfriends. Angelo was just one of them. But Sara wasn't pretty like her mother and the little girls at her new school didn't like her or make her feel welcomed on the other side of the country, in a state she only knew about from a first grade geography lesson.

And that's how it stayed. Sara in a new world that was too confusing with a mother that was too beautiful, who had too many boyfriends, and little Sara with not too many friends. In elementary school, it was just whispering behind her back or calling her names on the playground, or whenever Sara was standing in front of them, in the lunchroom, to get back in school after recess. They would pull her hair, sometimes hard, sometimes not so hard, but always, through all of this, it would make her cry. One time, on the *playground, the name-calling got so bad, Sara peed her pants—and the whole class laughed.*

In middle school, it got much worse. The bullying followed her off the school grounds and travelled all the way to the internet and called her worse names and pulled her hair even harder and made her cry stronger tears than ever she could have imagined in real life when they were standing right beside her.

I hear whispering down the hall, Andrea's room. It's four rooms away. I stand by her door to see if I can recognize the voices. It's Amanda. I'm sure. I can't figure out what they're saying. But I stand by the door anyway and listen. I'm curious what they're doing, but I can't seem to find the guts to walk in.

Amanda and Andrea, the twins from *Alice in Wonderland*, they sort of remind me of. Or maybe it's more like the little girls from *The Shining*, both of them with longish, brown, pin-straight hair.

I think they've both been here for a while. I'm not sure how long, but I get the feeling they've both settled into this hospital, like a good pair of shoes that you just can't seem to take off of your feet. Sometimes I get weirded out, the way that they're always whispering with their hands cuffed over their mouths. Sometimes, when I look at them, I think about those girls who used to pick on Sara. Martina and Stephanie, I think their names were. Sara would tell me how they were always whispering to each other when she was around, always looking her up and down and laughing. These girls would tell stories about her, stories you wouldn't even believe such young people like that could make up about another person; but they did. And the people in Sara's school, they believed them. Anyway, I'm just saying, sometimes, when I look over at Andrea and Amanda and all their whispering to each other, I can't help but think about those stories Sara used to tell and think, well, maybe, they're just like that. But, anyway,

I'm not sure I think that way anymore. Now I'm thinking it's not that they're being mean or anything but that they're just so scared to talk out loud to other people.

Sometimes in group, I look at them and all their crying and think they're both a little pathetic. They have all these attachments to other people. Sure, I have my issues, but it's people I hate the most. If I have to listen to one more story from Andrea about her boyfriend that used to beat her up and how much she thinks about how she *hurt* him, I feel like I'm gonna jump up on my feet and walk over to her and smack her as hard as I can to knock some sense into her. Forget about this man, I want to tell her. Forget about them all. They will suck you down into the blackest hole you could ever imagine existing in this universe, so far down, you'll never be able to pull yourself up.

"Hey Lissaahhhhh, what'cha doing?" I'm startled. I turn around quickly, afraid it's one of the nurses. But it's Allison. "What'cha spying on? Let's go in and see what they're doin' for ourselves," she says with a glass of ice in her hands.

"You're supposed to be sleeping," I say with a stern voice, though I have no idea why.

"Chill out, girl. Just went to get myself a cold refreshment. That bitch Jackie never does do a good job of watching over what she's supposed to be watching over and always leaves her little set of keys laying on top of that cheesy knock-off Gucci bag of hers. I suppose she tells herself everybody's *really* sleeping in here as she hangs outside all night on her cell phone, trying to give herself cancer."

"What are you talking about?"

"I'm talking about this little key ring, right here," she says, dangling that silver ring with about ten or so keys on it in front of my face.

"You want to go see what's inside. This thing will open up anything in this stupid little house. They got an ice machine and a little white refrigerator filled with Coke and Sprite and ice tea and everything you'd want in that office and another little white chest filled with some other stuff, if you know what I mean. That's what this little brass one's for." And she holds that key apart from the others, like she's trying to get me to go along with a sneaky little plan of hers.

And I know what she means, but I don't know what she's getting at. Does she expect me to go poking around that office with her looking to drop someone else's medication?

"What da ya say, Lisssaaahhhh? Jackie's been out there for hours, smoking like she's filling up a chimney. *You know* she's not coming in anytime soon, don't ya? And Margot's passed out. Let's go in the office and see what they've got in there. What da ya gotta to lose?"

"Yeah, whatever. Nothing else to do," I say, though I immediately regret it. I watch her open that door and let herself in like it's part of her normal routine.

I'm a little apprehensive. Yeah, the likelihood of either one of those nurses sneaking up on us without first hearing them come down the hallway this late at night is minute, but still, I can just imagine Dana's look of disappointment after she finds out I broke into their office. And even though that woman gets underneath my skin like a bad rash, that look in her eye when she wants you to realize her disapproval makes you feel as small as a squashed bug.

"Hey Chiquita, you want something to drink?"

"I'll have an ice tea, if they got any."

"One ice tea coming up. Hey Lisa, think fast." And with that brief warning, she chucks that can over at my head. Thankfully, my adrenaline's pumping so hard, I'm able to intercept it before it smashes into the metal filing cabinet.

"Allison, what the fuck are you doing? That could have woken everybody up. I'm going back."

"Don't get your panties into a bunch. Nobody's gonna come running in. I can hear that bitch out there still jabbering on that phone of hers, and trust me, Margot's out. Seriously, Lisa, you've gotta learn to chill the fuck out."

"Whatever," I say and decide to stay, purely out of boredom; there ain't nothing else to do except go to my room and stare at the ceiling.

This place. I don't think I've ever seen anything so neatly organized. Rows and rows of beige filing cabinets, all locked up against the wall, and mini boxes stacked along the desks, filled with index cards. I let my curiosity get the best of me and start looking through them. Allison's by the window going through Jackie's overnight bag, putting things down her pants. She's trying to be real slick, like I can't see what she's doing.

It's a list of medications. That's what the little boxes are for. Xanax. Desipramine. Percocet. Lithium. Divalproex. Abilify. No wonder why they all walk around like zombies.

Dana tries to push this crap down my throat too, but I usually just hold it under my tongue and spit it out when nobody's looking. If they had their way, they'd have me all drugged up and talking nonsense like my counterpart over here who's sitting in the corner mumbling some stupid song she doesn't know the words to and stinking up the room with someone else's perfume.

"Allison, don't you think someone's gonna smell that shit? It fucking reeks in here."

"What da ya think? It's too much, huh?"

"Yeah, just a little. Would you put that shit away?"

"It's some new shit by Jennifer Lopez. A little too sweet for me anyway. I guess I'll let her keep it for now."

"Don't you think she'll know that half her stuff is missing?"

"Who gives a shit? If she realizes anything, she'll just think it was Margot or one of the other nurses or something. She's never gonna come looking at me."

"Yeah. Whatever."

I just go back to my index cards because now curiosity has

gotten the best of me, and I can't wait to read the little notes they've got scribbled in the margins.

Amoxapine. Effexor. Prozac. Celexa. Lexapro. Paxil. Anger. Sadness. Hypersensitivity. Depression. Bipolar. ADHD. PTSD. OCD. Bulimia. Anorexia. Body Dysmorphia. Adderall. Dexedrine. Ritalin. Doxepin. Anxiety. Panic. Agoraphobia.

And, somewhat on purpose, I flip all the way down to the letter N, and even though she's only about five feet away, I just can't hold back the temptation to read the shit that's on Allison's little card. I try to be sly and peek over to ensure she's preoccupied, and then I sort out the rest of the cards, so that the one that says Newman is now in my field of view.

Addiction. Bipolar. Major Depressive Disorder. Insomnia. Restlessness. Weight Loss. Zoloft. Lamotrigine. Percocet. Cymbalta. Methadone. Trimipramine. Ambien. History of violent episodes towards herself and other people. Should never be trusted with a metal object. Room to be inspected on a bi-daily basis.

I just can't help but wonder what she's gonna do with all that shit she's got stuffed in her underwear.

When she's exhausted her little search through Jackie's bag, I watch her salivating over the medicine cabinet, sizing up those little white labels.

"Hey, Lisa. You ever take this stuff, lithium? You take about five, and you're on cloud nine. You want a couple?"

To be honest, I do think about what it would be like to take those pills. But a modest instinct I usually try to ignore reaches out of me and puts a hold on any mischievous thoughts I may be having. "No, Allison, not tonight. I'm not in the mood."

"Whatever. I think I'm gonna go with the perkeys anyway. Sun's gonna be coming up soon. I could use a little morning energy boost," she says, reaching into the cabinet and gobbling down a handful of those little blue pills like she couldn't get them in her body fast enough. As soon as she does, she finishes off with a big gulp of soda and then locks up the cabinet. "Well, I think I'm good for the night. What da ya say we go see if the girls are still up? I feel like I got lots of energy all of a sudden."

I can tell that any minute all those pills are gonna start kicking in, and I'm not sure what this girl is gonna do, so I'm thinking I'm gonna take my out before she gets me into any real trouble. I just say, "No, Allison. I'm actually getting a little tired all of a sudden," and let out a fake little yawn as loud as I can manage. "I'll catch you at breakfast."

"Whatever. Suit yourself," she says in a self-preoccupied manner. Then she turns back to the cabinet, looking for whatever else she can siphon, and I find my way to the door as quickly and as quietly as I can.

"Sometimes it hurt so much to put a needle in my arm, but I did it anyway.

"I wanted to die. Heroin was the only thing that made me want to wake up every day. It was the only thing that made me feel anything about life.

"When I was thirteen, I was molested by my older cousin. I told someone I thought I could trust, someone I thought was my friend, and she turned around and told other people. She denied it, of course, but the next day in school, I could hear people talking about me. They wouldn't even be quiet about it.

"A school therapist found out and told my mother, and they made me go to a meeting with them. When it was over, I felt like it was my fault.

"Afterwards, I was the whore that nobody wanted to associate with. And I remained that way for a long time. At least throughout the rest of the year. I was the slut of the eighth grade nobody wanted to be friends with."

I remember the way that saltwater felt as it was forcing itself inside my lungs. It was helplessness. I looked to the sky and saw nothing but blue. Not even a cloud. I'd never seen anything look so perfect. And I could hear, with such precision, the high-pitched sounds of children, the echo of their laughter bouncing over the turbid seawater, and the gulls in the air screaming, "Eek, eek, eek," as they circled around me. Those sensations never felt so acute. There was a heaviness in my arms as they struggled to keep me above water, trying desperately to pull me up, despite the enormity of the current that I just couldn't fight with my seven-year-old body. It was dragging me down, and in the back of my head, I just kept looking at the sky and saying, "No, no, no."

"Allison, do you think your mother encouraged you to be silent?"

"I didn't want to talk about it anyway. When I had to go to that meeting with my mother and the counselor, I hated it. I just wanted to get out of there so badly. They kept staring at me like I had done something wrong."

"How did you feel then?"

"Like I wanted to fly away and forget about everything. At the end, we were supposed to sign up for another meeting. I said I had to check my schedule, something about school, and then I would get back to her and tell my mother. But I never did."

"And how did that make you feel?"

"I was happy I didn't have to talk about it. I could finally forget."

"Do you think you could forget about something like that?"

"I don't think about it all the time anymore."

"Let's go back to your mother, Allison. It didn't make you angry that she ignored what happened to you, that she didn't stand up and defend you?"

"I'm not sure if I wanted that. I hated when everybody in school found out. It made me feel so small. I could tell what everybody was thinking. Like I was disgusting. Like there was something wrong with me. I couldn't imagine if my dad and my brother knew. I couldn't imagine them looking at me like that."

"Do you think that your dad and your brother would look

at you like that?"

"I don't know. Everybody else did."

One time in Dana's office, I saw a picture of Allison when she was in junior high. It was on Halloween. She had on this white dress with homemade looking wings, something her mother probably made with tissue paper and wire hangers. The glitter on her cheeks and her bleachy blonde hair made her eleven-year-old face look bright and innocent. Now she looks ragged, like an old piece of clothing that's been hidden on the bottom of your closet for way too long, that you would never want to put on again.

Even though she's full of unsolicited advice, she was pretty ticked last time I mentioned that maybe she should cut her hair. She has to get rid of those godforsaken dreadlocks. All I did was mention once that I think she would look cute with a shorter cut, and she was like "I'm not fucking cutting my hair," so I just shut up and decided to go back to minding my own business.

She's strange anyway. She gets mad so quickly for the stupidest things. Sometimes I see her sitting in the rec room by herself, and I'll go up to her and say, "What's up, Allison?" and she'll be like, "What the fuck do you want?" And other times, she'll just come into my room and spread out on my bed and start telling me her whole fucking life story. That's why I stay away. You never know with people like that. One day they're your friend, and the next day, they're doing some fucked up shit behind your back that you find out about months later.

I remember when Gerda was here, and we were all sitting around listening to her stories about living in a Nazi camp during World War II. I saw Allison, from across the room, crying, as Gerda was telling of being raped repeatedly by some of the guards. She was trying to keep it low key, but I'm sure she could tell that everybody knew. It was one of those really intense sobbing cries when it's hard for you to catch your breath, and no matter what you do, you can't seem to get yourself to calm down.

Gerda, you could tell that she is a writer. The words she chooses evoke so much imagery; it feels like you are right there with her watching from across the room in some cold cement cellblock as the guards come in one by one and hold her down. She told many stories, but for me and Allison, the stories about those guards are the ones that ran deepest through our souls. It made my body temperature drop and my stomach bunch up in a tight knot.

I remembered that day, at the end of the struggle, when I knew I would go down. Nobody could hear me. I was trying to force words to come out of my mouth, but there were no sounds, only me screaming like in a silent movie. My struggle getting weaker. Losing my breath. The air all escaping. Knowing I couldn't fight any longer. And then it was dark.

Thirteen

Sara didn't really talk much, but I remember one time she came into my room at night and told me in secret that she cut her wrists when she was thirteen, but it didn't work. I think she was trying to make me feel better or something. Sara was like that. She didn't talk much, but she was very comforting. Sometimes I would see her in the hallway like when I was going to a meeting or back to my room and without even saying hello or anything she would walk over and give me a hug and then just smile and walk away, without even saying anything. By the time I could even get her name out of my mouth, she was already halfway gone, still walking down the hall.

Anyway, I guess that time when she cut herself, they brought her to another hospital, and she stayed there for about a month. After she was home for a couple of days, she went on the computer to check her Facebook page, and there were postings from people in her school. And they weren't nice. There were messages that said it was better now that she was dead because nobody liked her, and she was always having sex with other peoples' boyfriends. Sara said that wasn't true. That there were just these girls that hated her, so they made up lies and told everybody else so everybody would hate her too. She said the worse thing about seeing all that stuff on Facebook was that she had to go to school the next day and see everybody again and face all those people who wrote it.

Sometimes when I'm sleeping, I see things in my dreams. I can see Sara and those girls at her school. They're in the hallway where everybody can see them, and the girls are laughing in a mean way and making others around them laugh. I am there on the side, watching. I can see Sara trapped in the middle. She is so scared she is peeing in her pants, and when she does that, the other people laugh harder, so she starts crying harder. One time, she pulled a knife from her pocket and slit her wrists right there in the middle of all those people in her school hallway. None of them do anything to help as if they don't care if she lives or dies, and there's little Sara bleeding all over the place. I get so scared I start screaming and screaming for somebody to help. Then, the next thing I know, the nurses are in my room. I'm sweating and soaking wet from all the tears. The nurses try to get me to calm down and then give me a Xanax, which I just pretend to take.

Fourteen

Sara, Sara as red as a rainbow with a broken balloon of a heart, threw herself off the roof of the hospital because she heard that people could fly but flew into the air like a million shiny pieces of rain, broken and exhausted and prepared to sleep forever.

Now the story comes back to her as she sits in her room, alone and quiet at midnight, her mind as loud as a bell. She can hear dried fingers turning thick paper and the hard distinct voice of an old man, a grandfather with a yellow beard too scratchy to kiss and a nicotine voice. He told her they could fly, long ago the people had wings, and she follows this voice back in her own memory and out through the door of her empty room, the one she shares with no one, out through the door where there is more space and dark clear light with cold marble floors under bare feet. She hears the voice again, coming to her from down the hall; again, it's hard and tired just like it sounded to her four-year-old ears, so she follows it with her mind travelling through just that direction, to only that voice as she walks with no shoes down the cold marble hallway.

"They flew like blackbirds up above with their wings shining against the blue up there."

Then the voice melts down deep into nothing and becomes lost to her, no more hard voice, no more grandfather. The sound is broken and he never returns, and the story she remembers now is written through lines of sadness and tears dripping, salty and sticky, broken people with missing wings that could no longer smell Africa; so now she remembers sadness as she looks through the black light on the cold floor and listens to silence, can hear the life of nothing and is missing the sound of her grandfather's voice, the voice of love, the voice of worn out cotton pajamas and flannel shirts laying together. The voice that closed a book and never came back to read it again. But now that's what she thinks about. She sees endings, pages being turned to the left but never to the right again. She sees light coming through an open window, light that looks clean and gentle, so she walks as close as she can get to it and opens the window and climbs like a spider to the roof until she gets to the top and lies her feet flat again. She sees light in front of her, light and stars and blue, peaceful baby blue like washed clothing, and light that was so clear, Sara wanted to run and jump and fly into the air like the people from Africa through the sound of her grandfather's dying voice.

Fifteen

"You would have been fine."

"No, I wouldn't have. I don't know how you can say that."

"You, Dad, and April would have been just fine. I'm sure you would have been embarrassed, but after a while, people would forget, and you would forget, and you would move on."

"I can't believe you would say that. Why do you think I don't love you?"

"Please. Are we making this about you? Of course, somehow, you would find a way to make this about you."

Lisa looked up at Dana expecting her to interrupt, to tell her mother what she should say next. But she didn't. She just looked at them and waited for one of them to break and start talking, to each other. And it was Rosemary, but she looked at Dana and not at Lisa.

"Why is this my fault? You're both looking at me like this is my fault. Okay. I'm a horrible mother. My daughter had a problem. My daughter was depressed. And I didn't do anything about it. Goddammit, Lisa, all teenagers look sad sometimes. And you were always mad at me. Always. How was I supposed to know something was really wrong? You never told me anything. You could've come to me, but you didn't. You always ran to your room and locked the door so nobody could talk to you. And that's my fault. You lock the door and give everyone the silent treatment, and that's my fault."

"You're a fucking liar."

"Excuse me?"

"You're a fucking liar. I told you I was unhappy. I asked you to take me out of that school, to let me switch schools and let me go to St. Patrick's. And you said no. And now you're lying."

"I didn't say no, Lisa."

"Yes, you did. You're lying."

"No, I didn't. I said maybe just give it time, and if you were still unhappy in the summer, we could talk about it for next year. I didn't say no."

"Next year. You said we would talk about it next year. What was I supposed to do until then?"

"We talked about it. I told you there was a therapist at school. You said you were going to talk to him. You said that you did. That you talked to him. That things were better. Okay. Fine. You said that things were fine."

"Things were fine, mother. That's what everybody says when they're trying to blow somebody off."

"Lisa, you want me to know everything. What do you want me to say? You have to blame me for everything, but you could have said something too. You could have told me. I wouldn't have sent you away. But you didn't. You didn't say anything. You always just walked away from me or ignored me."

"You're my mother. You should have known. I asked you to take me out of that school. I asked you. I pleaded with you. And you didn't. You said no. And then I hated you. I hate you. You're my mother, and I fucking hate you."

"This is not my fault, Lisa. You should have said something."

"I hate you. If you would have let me go, this wouldn't have happened. But you didn't help me."

Lisa was shaking. Something was different now. Something changed about her. She was different than the scared girl who wouldn't talk before.

Dana looked at her. "What wouldn't have happened?"

"Nothing. Leave me alone. I want to get out of here."

"What wouldn't have happened, Lisa?"

"Nothing. Fuck you. I hate you too."

"This is not my fault," her mother repeated. "How am I supposed to help you like this? See, you keep everything to yourself. Secrets. Secrets. Secrets. But you won't tell me. You won't tell Dana. If you don't tell us, how are we supposed to know?"

"They wouldn't leave me alone, but you could have stopped

them if you let me go. But they wouldn't. They wouldn't stop. Why wouldn't they leave me alone?"

"Lisa, who wouldn't leave you alone?" Dana asked.

"Josh and Paul. They wouldn't leave me alone. They would never leave me alone. They were just everywhere. They always said that I was ugly. That nobody wanted me. They made everybody laugh at me, at school, because of them."

Lisa got up and walked over to the wall and stared at the picture of the weeping willow tree. Then, she looked back at Dana and then her mother. Tears fell out of her eyes, hard like heavy glue. She just looked out away from everything and spoke to herself. "Nobody helped me."

"Lisa," her mother said.

"Nobody helped me. Everybody just let me cry. They let them attack me."

"They attacked you?" Dana asked, a little afraid of what Lisa would admit. She knew there was trouble at school. She knew that Lisa was having trouble with kids at school, that that was the reason she was so angry, but it hit her now, when Lisa said that word, attacked, that something else had happened; there was something that went deeper than just the name calling and the taunting. "How did they attack you, Lisa?"

"Nothing. Leave me alone." Lisa turned around and looked back at the picture of the weeping willow tree. There was a tree like that over by the woods of her school. She could see it out the window in the back of the gym locker room. It was the first thing she saw when she ran back up the hill from Josh and Paul. Now she just looked at the tree trapped behind the glass picture frame. It was supposed to look pretty. That's why it was there. That's why Dana put it on the wall, under the glass, because it was supposed to look pretty. But it didn't. To Lisa, it looked trapped and perverted. It made her sick. It made her want to throw up.

"Lisa, how did they attack you?" Dana asked again.

"Shut up." She turned back to look at her mother. "I hate you. I hate you. If you would have let me go, you could've stopped them. But you didn't."

"How did they attack you, Lisa?"

Lisa turned back to the wall to look at the picture again and somehow got lost inside of it. "I fucking hate you. I fucking hate both of you. If you would have taken me away from there, that tree would still look pretty."

Her mother didn't say anything. She was scared now. She was scared to say anything, and she was scared what Lisa would say. She wanted to put her hands up to her ears before Lisa said anything else. She just watched her look at that tree in the picture frame and hoped that was it. That she wouldn't say one more thing that day. That the session would end. That the day would be over.

"Lisa," Dana asked again. "How did they attack you?"

"You should have taken me away from there. You were my

mother. You should have protected me, but you didn't. And they fucking raped me. You stupid, selfish bitch. They fucking raped me and now they won't let me go." And before anybody could think about what was happening or what to say next, Lisa lifted her hands up and pulled that picture off the wall and threw it against the wall on the other side of Dana's office, until it smashed into a million shiny pieces of glass thrown all over the carpet.

Denise Dragiewicz

Part II

Sixteen

Lieutenant James Scagglia had been home for five years before he met his wife, a young waitress from a bar he used to frequent on the Lower East Side each day at 5:30 when his shift at the Local 513 had ended. He brought little home with him and lived in a basement studio with his German Shepherd, Duke, and a pull-out couch the two slept on. His surroundings meant little, and so he was fine with a few old pots from the Salvation Army he used to boil coffee and fry eggs for breakfast. In the nightstand beside the couch was a small leather pouch filled with the only thing he had taken back from the war, aside from his uniform that was packed away in the closet.

Laura was six years younger, the grandchild of Italian immigrants who grew up in the Bronx. It was a small ceremony with only the bride's father and James' good friend from the local there to witness the two become man and wife.

James moved up at his job when he learned to weld so the two moved out of the basement and into an apartment that had a *larger room and was above the ground, which was good, for the doctor told James it would be bad for the baby and for Laura to spend too much time in a humid environment. That was okay. James wanted her and their child to be happy and comfortable and, most importantly, healthy. He continued to visit the bar every day at 5:30 until the baby grew too large inside of Laura, and the doctor said it was better to stop working and stay off of her feet; and so for the next two months, until Laura gave birth, James came home with a six-pack of his own and kept Laura company. Sometimes, James would wake in the night and watch Laura next to him, quiet and peaceful. He would rub his hands over the top of her large belly and imagine what the baby would look like and what it would feel like for him to hold it and wonder if the baby would like to be held by him. He thought, soon, soon, the baby will be born, and I'll be able to sleep through the night.*

She came suddenly one day when Laura was cooking. James had just gotten home, and Laura was frying pork chops in an iron skillet when her water broke, and she was standing over a puddle in the kitchen. James grabbed her bag and the two of them took a taxi to St. Vincent's where the baby was born in less than two hours. James stayed with her the entire time, holding her hand and helping her breathe. His trepidation kept his excitement at bay, but in those two hours waiting for his child to be born, James felt a quiet, relaxed feeling inside that he hadn't known for so long, that he had forgotten ever existed. But during those moments, he remembered. He remembered playing baseball as a teenager and feeling the same way before a game. He was the all-county pitcher with a winning record, and because he so often led his team to victory, he seldom thought of apprehension or fear like most of his teammates. His confidence was enough to make him quiet on the inside, so quiet that nothing on the outside really mattered, and he could hear the voice inside of him say everything was going to be just fine. That same feeling and same voice was with him in the delivery room, and he knew that when the baby came, the three of them would be happy.

It was a girl and after forty-eight hours in the hospital, the three of them were allowed to leave. At first, everything was just as James had imagined during that quiet time at the hospital. But after a few days of sleeping, the baby woke up and began to cry and cry so much through the morning and through the night that it became the only sound that James ever heard when he was in that apartment. And even though he loved the baby and he loved his wife, there was just something about the crying that was too much for James to handle, and so at 5:30 after his day at the local was over, James began to go back to that little dive in the lower part of Manhattan even though Laura was no longer there. He would come home too late at night to spend too much time with his wife and wake up in the morning when the apartment was quiet and the two of them had just fallen asleep and sneak out to go to work and stay gone for the whole day. And this is how it stayed between the two of them until the baby was one and five months, and Laura started to get tired, too tired to care for the baby, and so James brought her to the hospital where the doctor said, "There's nothing we can do. The cancer has spread too much." In two months, Laura would be gone, and it would just be James and the baby in that small apartment on the Lower East Side.

Laura's sister slept on the couch for the final three weeks of Laura's life, but after the funeral, she had to go back to her own family, and so James and the baby only had each other. And when they were alone and the baby would cry, James would leave her in her crib and stare from outside in the hallway, unable to go near her. Eventually, they moved to the suburbs so the baby's aunt could take care of her. And then James stayed away. When he came home from the local, he would walk past his sister-in-law's house and just keep walking. The crying was too much. And before the baby was two years old, he went looking through his old things from the war and found his brown leather pouch, the only thing that would quiet the sound of the baby's cry that he always carried with him.

Sister

You don't look like me,

But I cry like you,

For you, in the sadness

I can't see; but I can feel

Pain below the skin.

Let me take, at least half,

So we share a resemblance,

And people will know,

That we are part of each other.

Seventeen

"They raped me," Lisa said to Sara. "They trapped me between them, and they wouldn't let me go. I never told anyone that before."

"Who were they?"

"Two boys at school. They hate me, but I never thought they would do that. I was never really afraid until that happened. Afterwards, I couldn't get them off me. I could still feel them on my body, like they were inside of me, and they wouldn't let me go. I can still feel them with me now. Why can't I get away from them?"

"You can't," Sara said. "They're in you now, and they'll stay with you forever. Once they go inside of you, you can never get them out."

Lisa knew on some level that could be true. But she couldn't stand it. She couldn't stand the thought of Josh and Paul being inside of her forever. She hated them. Before, she had feared them, but now it was just hatred. The fear had settled inside of her in the weeks being away from school, and when Dana told her she didn't have to go back there, that she could switch schools, it took a while, but it relaxed her inside, and she began to let go of the fear that had taken hold of her at the beginning of her freshman year when Paul and Josh first became friends and decided they would build their power by destroying her own. Now, anger took over, and the thought of them staying with her forever, like Sara warned, just made her think of hating them even more. She felt sick. Throw-up welled inside of her stomach, and she suddenly felt like she wanted to puke up everything that she had been holding inside of her, everything that was making her sick.

"You can never get rid of it," Sara repeated. "Once they're inside of you, they never let you go."

"I want to let them go, Sara. I don't want them to be with me all of the time."

"He's with me all the time. I can always feel him. He smelled like whiskey, like sticky whiskey and sweat, and I can smell that whiskey and feel that sweat with me always."

But Sara's sadness was different than Lisa's. There was an acceptance inside of her that life would always be sad. She was more than the broken guitar string that could be replaced. With her, it was as if the frame had been torn out. And even with repair, the sweet music that came from her instrument at one time would never ring as sweet or as gentle. There would always be something offbeat or awkward to the rhythm of her world. And she accepted that defeat. Learned that was the only way she could open her eyes in the morning, to suck up that sadness like the stale air of a balloon and hold it down within herself until it was so far down it just rested deep inside of her and made a permanent home.

"I don't want them with me forever," Lisa said again. "Let's try, Sara, to make them go away." Lisa hadn't touched the body of another human being in months, but she reached over and took Sara's hand and held it tightly within her own.

I want to sunbathe under arctic deserts,

Frozen skies,

Bare feet and gloveless hands.

I want to slide across ice-coated carpets,

Lose all sensation in

My frostbitten fingers;

Paralyze my thoughts and recollections

In uninhabitable breezes.

I want to close my eyes under plastic goggles,

Cover my flesh in polar bear jackets,

Freeze my thoughts and numb my memories—

Forget that I am settled on

A latitude of languishment.

Eighteen

Sometimes I think about what it could be like living as another person, in a different body, a totally different life with different parents, in a different school, in some foreign city on a distant continent. Sometimes I think Barrow, Alaska. It's the most northwest you can go above the Arctic Circle in our country. Or maybe Antarctica. In Antarctica, you have to live underground for most of the year. And for most of the year, there is no way to get off that continent. You're just stuck there alone, with very few people. I bet you, in many ways, that's the most isolated place on the planet. You know, if I could be any other person, I think I would be a researcher who lived down there and studied bird migrations or global warming or some shit like that. I wish I was that person. I wish I was anybody else than me, stuck in some old hospital with cold marble floors that reek of chlorine bleach and make the whole place feel toxic and contaminated.

"Hey there, Shakespeare. Everybody's all lined up for the buses. Dana said, 'Allison, go get Lisa. She's late aa-gg-aaainnn.'

So here I am. But we can take our time. I love to get her little panties in a bunch anyway. So what's ya working on today, Shakespeare? Written any sonnets lately?"

I hate her fucking bullshit. With Allison it can never just be, "Hi Lisa. It's time to go. Everybody's waiting for you." There always has to be some dramatic edge to magnify even the most unimportant detail. But I just ignore her little antagonisms and say, "Yeah. Let me just put my stuff away. I'll be right there."

"No problemo. I'm just the messenga," she says as a wad of pink bubblegum protrudes out of her mouth and blows the most obnoxious bubble I've ever seen. I walk right passed her swinging against the doorframe in the rec room, watching every move I make as I go to put my journal down. She's waiting for me. I thought she was just the "messenga," but now she's gonna be the escort as well. I look over to her as I slowly take my time to put my things away; she stands there and watches and gives me a furtive little wink as if she knows exactly what I'm doing, and she's slightly amused by it.

"Go ahead, Lisa. Take all the time you want. I can picture Dana waiting there for us in that bus, tapping that pen so hard against her notebook, little plastic chips splattering all over the place, making a mess. Love it. Don't pretend you don't love it too. You know exactly what buttons to push. I've been paying attention, taking notes."

"Dana's not that bad. I'm not trying to fuck with her," I

say as I close the door to my room and walk out in front of her, just to give her the impression I don't have any intention of spending the day by her side. But she quickly catches up and throws her arm around my shoulder like we are best buddies. I just look off into the distance and ignore her every move.

"You know, girl, I got some special treats to take with us on our little excursion. You interested?"

I stop and look at her, and before I can let a word out of my mouth, she looks back at me with one of her winks and slides a little pill into my left hand. I don't even look at it before I slide it into my pocket and shake my head at her as if to express some type of gratitude although I'm not sure what the fuck she just gave me or why I should be grateful to her for anything. But that's that.

Everybody's on the bus, and to Allison's credit, Dana *is* there in that front seat looking frantic and pissed off, and, of course, tapping that pen against her stack of folders like we just made her late for an important meeting or something. On the bus, there are few empty seats, and thank God none of them are together. Allison jumps into the first one she sees; then she spreads out with her hands folded under that rat's nest of hers and gives out a great big yawn, so that everybody can notice her, as if they didn't just watch her walk onto the bus. I proceed to walk past her little presentation, grateful to be rid of her, at least for the hour and forty-five minutes it should take to get to the horse farm, but she turns her head and yells down the aisle, "Hey Lissaaahhh, enjoy the riiiddde," with that obnoxious little extended vowel sound of hers.

Somehow there is a window seat open in the back, sitting there, waiting just for me. There's some new girl sitting in the left seat who seems very familiar though we've never spoken, and I'm so not looking forward to meeting a "new friend" and listening to her life story all the way to the farm. Here there are too many stories. I walk over and gesture like I want to get over by the window, and she just grins and lets me in. "I'm Carrie," she says with a brief smile, seeming a little too intimidated to talk too much. I look back and say, "I'm Lisa," with only a nod, implying that I'm content to leave the conversation there for the moment. And she doesn't push it, which makes me happy.

As the bus pulls out, I look out the side window and ignore all the chitchat I hear around me. I think more and more about that little pill that's in my pocket and how Allison got it and what the fuck it would do to me and whether or not I should put it in my mouth.

Fuck it. This is going to be a group cooperation weekend. If I have to deal with this bullshit, I might as well be stoned in some sense or another. I pop it into my mouth and close my eyes to block everything out, as best as I can anyway.

And I must have dozed off, because the next thing I know Carrie's waking me up. I open my eyes and look out the window. We're in some rural area with lots of maple trees. There's an old red barn in the distance behind a large horse pen that must hold a couple dozen of those things and some smaller cottages spread out on the farm. I wonder if this is a guest farm like where people stay when they go on vacation. Today there's no one but us.

"Lisa, are you going to join us?" Dana calls to me, getting impatient for the second time this morning. I can tell she's pissed by the high-pitched sound of her voice, like fingernails being drawn across a chalkboard. She waits for me at the head of the bus. "Is there something I need to know about, Lisa? What's going on this morning?"

"Nothing. I'm just tired. I didn't get enough sleep. You know how it goes."

"Well maybe I should prescribe you something for that, Lisa. It's not healthy for you to stay up so often at night."

"It's fine, Dana. It's getting better, my sleep, really. I'm good with the drugs for now."

"Well, you look awful. Your eyes are all bloodshot."

And then I remember that shit I dropped about an hour ago.

"Are you going to be okay today?"

"Yeah, yeah. Let's just go and get on with it," I say as I blow past her and quickly go outside to join the others.

The window is open and the air outside is filled only with gray light and a static smell that takes the pleasure out of breathing, but suddenly Lisa's senses move her mind as she breathes in a smoky scent coming from the parking lot. It is not the sweet aroma of smoke that she is used to, not the thick pungent smell of a joint or the dense favorable hit off of a glass pipe, sweet and invigorating, even though she presses her hand hard to her upper chest to prevent her breath from releasing the smoke too quickly. No, now, this is an unwanted smoke, a gassy smoke, a smoke that makes you choke or think of being stuck on summer highways with car exhaust that makes the air look wavy and distorted.

The toxic air is all Lisa needs to bring her back to her own lurid memories. She moves closer to the window, wanting to inhale the thick, polluted stream of gas, trying to suffocate her thoughts with soft, deep, almost passionate breaths of poison. She doesn't want to go back to eighth period when she didn't go to gym, when she walked out the back door after attendance, when the teacher wasn't looking, and the girls were choosing each other for their volleyball teams. Just before, as she pressed her hand into the back pocket of her gym shorts, she felt a joint, still rolled up tightly from last week, after class, when she took a few drags in the locker room just as the sound of the bell scattered all the girls and all the teachers so no one would have time to think about the direction of the smoke.

She remembers the feeling of the joint and the smoke flowing through her and thinks of going down into the tunnels that are not far from the gym's back door. She is standing with her palm in her back pocket, rolling around the semi-smoked joint with the bottom tips of her right fingers, almost tasting its sweet stickiness in her mouth. Nobody notices as she walks through the door that is cornered open to allow the cool January air to circulate through the gym.

Outside, Lisa walks into the moist, dewy grass and arches her feet to the side as she glides down a miniature hill to enter into the untamed woods at the back end of the school where there are tunnels that are too intricate for the security to bother with.

But before she can spark the flint from her pink plastic lighter, she feels the air of cigarette smoke blow in from the other direction and knows she is not alone. As the smoke moves closer, she inhales the fumes, almost as if they are curled up tightly between her two fingers and pressing against her lips; but the voices walking towards her through the dusty air quickly dismiss any senses related to the pleasure of smoking and instead infuse a sense of panic and immobility around her as she realizes that Josh and Paul will soon be standing in front of her before she has the chance to run.

She feels the wall of her stomach collapse and heat take over her body, extinguishing any sense of relaxation she thought about as she left through the gym doors, only moments before. She knows for sure, as her senses come together, and the voices become more distinct, that the boys will soon be close to her.

Now, it is laughter coming towards her, echoing like the

malevolent sound of a clown from a movie she is not supposed to be watching. Horror, that's what it feels like to be trapped, even by voices in empty tunnels she can run back through, quickly, so they wouldn't see her, and she can go, back up the hill and run through the field through the back of the school, so she would be caught by the guards, and she would spend next week, every day, after school. That was all right, and that was her chance, but voices too quickly become the loose gravely sound of footsteps and eyes come out of the darkness and see her standing there alone.

"You're mad at your mother."

"Whatever, Dana. It's fine."

"Lisa, you seem pretty angry with her. Not just yesterday, but you have said on many occasions that you blame your mother for putting you in danger."

"So, you do too."

"I didn't say that, Lisa. I'm only trying to understand how you feel."

"You just said she put my life in danger."

"I asked you if that's what you think. Do you think she left you in high school to get bullied, like she turned her back on you?"

"What do you think?"

"It doesn't matter what I think. I want to know how you feel, Lisa, how you feel about your mother."

"Dana, of course I'm pissed at her. I told you. I told her. Why do I have to repeat myself? Yes, she fucking left me in that school when I asked her to take me out, and she knew I was unhappy. People don't come home crying every day when they're happy."

"You sound angry now, Lisa."

"Of course I'm fucking angry, Dana. Can we cut the fucking bullshit? I asked her to take me out. But she made me stay. So I swallowed a bottle of painkillers. Fuck her. Fuck everybody else."

"Did you do it for revenge, Lisa, to get back at her?"

"No, I did it to fucking kill myself."

"And the decision to do that had nothing to do with her?"

"No, actually, it had to do with me, Dana, and the fucking miserable life I have. When I decided to kill myself, it had nothing to do with anyone. Only me. It's my life, and I have the right to end it if I want to. I mean, fuck you and fuck my mother. You guys don't know fucking anything. You have no idea what I went through. What life was like for me. This is all fucking bullshit. You want me to change my mind and say that I'm sorry and say I have hope that life could be better. But that's a lot of fucking BS. I know life. It doesn't get fucking better. It only gets worse. You think I want to wait and see how much more miserable I can be. No thank you."

"Now you're angry. I'd rather see this side of you. I want to hear why you're so upset."

"You're so fucking full of shit. You're trying to trap me or trick me into saying something. My mother's probably hiding underneath the desk or something, listening to everything."

"Your mother's not here, Lisa. Why would you think I would trick you? Or trap you? That's an interesting word. Do you feel like people try to trap you in life?"

"Dana, I fucking hate you right now."

"Why is that, Lisa?"

"Why are you doing this to me?"

"Because I'm trying to help you."

"You're trying to trick me."

"Lisa, what do you mean by that? How would I be trying to trick you?"

"You want me to say something. You want me to say I'm sorry or to take it back."

"No, Lisa. I don't want you to say you're sorry. I want to hear this side of you. I want to know why you're so angry."

"I'm angry because everybody is trying to hurt me."

"You really think that's true about everybody? What about the girls? What about Sara? Do you think she was trying to hurt you?"

"Sara's dead now, so it doesn't fucking matter."

"And how does that make you feel?"

"What kind of stupid question is that?"

"I don't think it's a stupid question. Sara killed herself. That has to make you feel certain things. The two of you were getting really close."

"And it didn't matter, did it? She's dead now. She fucking jumped off the roof of the hospital. And now I'm alone again."

"You're not alone, Lisa."

"Yes, I am. If she loved me, she would have stayed with me. I thought we were going to do this together. She promised she would do this with me, but she's dead now."

"What did she promise you, Lisa?"

"She knew how I felt. She told me. She told me, these two

girls, they made everybody hate her. They put signs around the school, in the bathrooms, in the boy's and girl's bathrooms, that said she was a whore. That even in ninth grade, when she was only fourteen, they put signs up saying that she was having sex with the boys in her gym class, in the locker room. They wrote names, and the boys didn't deny it. They said that it was true. That she was sleeping with them. And they even wrote it on their Facebook pages, to stay away from Sara because she was a whore, and she had genital herpes. And nobody would talk to her, especially in gym, when she was changing in the locker room. Nobody would go near her, like they were afraid to get a disease she didn't even have. That's why she didn't go back to high school. She just ran away the day that school was supposed to start."

"Did she tell you how she got here, why she decided to kill herself?"

"She told me when she got to New York, she was lost. She just got on a bus and got off a bus and that was it. She walked around with her backpack on for over a day, just walking around a city she had only been to once to see a play when she was nine. She just walked around, afraid to stop anywhere, afraid to go to sleep, until she found a group of kids at the park. They went up to her and said she could crash with them if she wanted. So she did. She lived like that in a sleeping bag for months. When it started to get cold, her and about fifteen other kids got a cheap apartment in Harlem. She even told me some of the other people she lived with, they slept with people for money. Even some of the boys. And some of them used to smoke crack, and she would watch them."

"Did Sara ever do anything like that?"

"Yes, she slept with some older guys when she was there, for money once. But she was afraid. She said, she only did it one time. She couldn't do it again. She didn't want me to tell anyone. But I guess it doesn't matter anymore."

"And when did she leave? How did she finally get home to her mother?"

"One day in the winter, the cops followed some kids back to their apartment after they tried to sell drugs and busted all of them. When they found out who she was and that she was only fifteen, they sent her back to her mother."

"And then what happened? Did she get along with her mother? Was she happy at all to be back home?"

"She never really said anything about her mother. I'm not sure. I don't think she was a bad mother. I just don't think either one of them ever talked much to each other. But she said they made her go back to school in January. And that her mother walked her there to make sure she would go, even walked her into her first class. Everyone remembered who she was, and they all laughed at her, especially when they saw her mother walk her to class. She tried not to look back at them, but she could see everybody look at her and hear them whisper. And that's how it was all day. Through all nine periods. During lunch, she hid in the bathroom, but during her other classes, they made sure she was there. And the whole day, nobody talked to her. They just stared at her and told secrets about her. Secrets that she could hear."

"And what happened after that, Lisa? Did she tell you what she did?"

"She said she wouldn't do it again. That she wouldn't go back to being trapped the way she was before. But they wouldn't let her out. Her mother. The school. They were going to make sure she stayed. So after school, instead of getting on the bus, she walked down to the highway and walked out in front of a car. She was in the hospital for three weeks before they brought her here."

"And how does that make you feel?"

"I think she was stupid."

"Why?"

"Because she could've done something easier. She could've used a knife or taken some pills like I did. It works for a lot of people, you know. She always does these stupid things. First the car. Then the roof. There are other ways. She didn't have to do it like that."

"She didn't have to do it *at all*, Lisa."

"Of course she did. What else was she going to do?"

"She could've tried to get help. She could have tried to talk to somebody."

"Right. You make everything seem so easy, Dana. But

that's not really the way things work, and I think you know that too. You know you're full of shit."

"Lisa."

"No. Talking? What the fuck did that ever do for me? I talked to some shrink at my school, and he did jack shit. You know, I tried to tell him what happened, and he did nothing. He made it seem like it was my fault, like it was something I had to cope with. That's what he fucking told me. I had to learn to cope with my own problems. But I told him about Josh and Paul and the other kids who were giving me a hard time, and he did nothing. They're the ones who should have gotten into trouble. He should have done something to them. But he didn't. He should have reported it, but he didn't."

"He should have done something, Lisa."

"But he didn't. And what about Allison? She told a friend of hers, a close friend of hers, that her cousin raped her, and what does she do? She tells the whole fucking school. And the therapist she told didn't do jack shit either. And her mother, as far as I'm concerned, stabbed her in the back too, just like my mother did to me."

"Is that what you think, Lisa? That she stabbed you in the back?"

"Oh my God, we're going to go back to this now. The one fucking thing I don't want to talk about."

"Why don't you want to talk about it?"

"You know why."

"No, I don't, Lisa. I don't know enough."

"You want to know why, Dana?"

"Yes, Lisa, I do."

"And then you'll stop fucking asking me?"

"Yes."

"Because she was my mother. You know, when I was little, she used to tell me that she loved me. She used to read me a book every night before I fell asleep, and before she turned my light out, she kissed me on the forehead and told me she loved me. And I believed her."

"Of course you believed her, Lisa, and I know she did. I know, even now, I know she loves you."

"Bullshit. She told me she loves me, but she's a fucking liar. You can't love somebody and not see them. You can't love somebody and ignore them. I cried all the time. Why didn't she know that? I wanted her to see me, but she didn't."

"And do you think if she would have seen you, if she knew that you were crying, and she tried to help, that you wouldn't have tried to kill yourself?"

"I don't know. I don't know what would have happened. I just wanted somebody to help me. I thought she would have. I thought she would have helped me, but she didn't. You don't know what it's like not to be loved, but I do. Sara did. Allison does. The only person here who ever knew love is Amanda, and her mother is dead. And now she's alone anyway, so who really gives a shit about this bullshit we have to go through every day. Sara was the only one who was strong. She did what we all wished we could do."

"Lisa, you don't really mean that though. I know you don't."

"You don't know how I feel."

"No, I don't. But something tells me there is hope inside of you."

"I don't know. I don't know if there is."

"Try to find it, Lisa. There is no hope for Sara now. She's gone. There's nothing we can do. But you can be different."

It was too exhausting watching another person die, even though later in their marriage there were moments when he was unsure of whether he loved her. Cancer was different than watching a group of men walk over a landmine, but in the end, he would still be looking at a corpse, a body he too vividly remembered as breathing. And the sound of a child who wouldn't stop crying made his three tours of duty in Vietnam seem vivid and pungent, all coming back to him at a force he could not defeat. Weeks after he buried his wife, all those sounds of burning children from the Batangan village played like harrowing music in his head that he could not unplug or shut off until he went back into the drawer where he locked away his things from the war and found that brown leather pouch that had all he needed to feel quiet again. And again, after all those years of being sober, all those voices and all those memories fell silent as soon as the drugs mixed into his bloodstream. So how could he go back to the baby and the sound he could not listen to without going crazy? One day, when he dropped her off at Laura's sister's, he never came back to pick her up and never picked up the phone or answered the doorbell after work. And then, eventually, she knew. Dana's father wasn't going to come back to pick her up. She was going to raise her. And that was okay. Husbands cannot raise babies without wives, and she knew that.

On the way home from his local, when he got off the train, sometimes he would walk past Laura's sister's and really think about going in. But then he would hear her cry through the living room window and knew that if he went to take the baby, that sound would eventually break him, so he left her there and never came back until she was eight years old, and he went to the house to drop off a present for Dana's communion in the morning before work, when he was sure everybody was sleeping, just to leave something on the porch that his daughter would open later in the day without him. It was a present that belonged to her that her mother would want her to have. He just couldn't give it to her himself. Couldn't bring himself to look into his grown-up daughter's face and see the eyes of his dead wife staring back at him. So he left the present on the porch and he went to work and then he went home and took out his pouch again for the last time. He knew he would never again take it out of his drawer, so he took out all the white powder he had left. Then he went into the garage and into his car, turned on the engine, fixed a needle, and laid his head back into the leather seat of his Firebird where the voices of the children would be quieted forever.

Nineteen

There's an old man over there trying to gather us together with a megaphone like we're at some speedway rally. His voice doesn't reveal it, at least over that megaphone, but physically he looks very old, with deep lines and wrinkles that saturate his face, making it, in a way, almost uncomfortable to look at.

It's funny how I can be so aware of things like that. I hate the way looks make people act so stupid. At school, there is this group of perfect looking girls who God must have designed after the Barbie Doll era, and they only hang out together, only with each other. And even though they are all stuck up and secretly everybody hates them, outwardly, they are who everybody wants to be with, in one way or another. They are arrogant, and they walk over everyone like somehow a higher power infused them with a God-given right to hurt feelings and ruin reputations. But yet they get the attention of the whole school just because it looks like their faces belong on the cover of *Teen Vogue*, and people who don't look like that, they get stepped on all over.

Anyway, I try to block all that stupidity out of my head as long as I am forced to play a part on this earth. I try to pretend that looks don't matter and that the last thing I would ever do is act like those stupid assholes at my school who go around all day and suck up to people who are blank inside where it should really matter, but then I hear myself judging other people just by their appearance and realize I'm just like the rest of them. We're all a rotten bunch, all of differing degrees, but sometimes I think we're no one better than another.

"Lisa. Hello. Do you need to go someplace and lie down for a little while?"

"No, Dana. I'm fine. Just taking in the scenery."

"Uh hugh," she says, looking me up and down like she's on to me for some reason, but she doesn't know exactly what it is. "Well, you're with our group today. All of you will be sleeping together in Cottage C. Here is the schedule for our meals. Dinner is at 6:00 pm sharp, Lisa. Do you think you can manage that?"

"Yes, Dana."

"Okay. Then go and meet the others and let them know, and I'll see you at dinner. They're giving you a boxed lunch for the trails."

And I take it that's her final piece of instruction, and I start heading away. Then she reaches out with her right hand to pull me back as if she wants to tell me something in secret. "Lisa, I need you to keep an eye on Allison while we are here, especially tonight when you're alone. I don't trust her not to get herself and the rest of you into a little bit of trouble. I know it's not fair of me to ask that of you, but I'm asking anyway. Would you do that for me?"

"Yeah, sure, Dana, of course. I'll do whatever I can." And again I turn away and try to make a run for it when she pulls me back for a second time.

"Lisa, try to have some fun today. You'll like horseback riding. I know you will. Just be sure to give that horse a little bit of your trust, and he'll treat you just fine. You know, Lisa, I picked this activity with you in mind, because I thought it would cheer you up," she says to me looking all sentimental. It makes me feel a little bit awkward hearing all this honesty coming out of Dana for a change. I kind of don't know how to respond to it. "Just go have fun, okay?"

"Yeah, I'll have fun, Dana. Don't worry," I say with a little smile, and then I start making my way towards the others with some bullshit to-do list in my hand that I guess it's now up to me to explain. I have to hand it to her. The woman is sly. For all her sentimental bullshit, she sure hopped a shitload of crap on my back that I now have to take care of.

Doesn't everybody have dreams when they wake up in a pool of their own tears? Apparently not. Recently, I was having a conversation with a nurse at the hospital, and I brought up a bad dream I had a few nights before. I mentioned that it was "one of those" dreams where I was crying so hard, that when I woke up, my face was soaked and swollen and the pillow and bedding around my head drenched. The trauma I was experiencing in my dream was so intense, it was physically making its way into the real world. To me, this was not unusual. Having "crying dreams" is something I have experienced all my life, at least since I can remember.

"Was it the first time you ever tried?"

"I guess for real it was. I drank a bottle of gin from my parents' liquor cabinet once, as much as I could, before I passed out. Then I woke up and got really sick. It was horrible. What about you, Sara?"

"Yes, when I was thirteen."

"What did you do?"

"I slit my wrists in the bathroom with a piece of glass. But my mother found me and brought me to the hospital."

"Was it a hospital like this?"

"Yes, but there were more people, but I didn't mind. I just stayed there for a month until they thought I was better and then they let me out. I got out of going to school for a month, so that was cool...did you ever kiss a boy, Lisa?"

"Just once."

"Only once?"

"Yes. I wanted to more. I just never did."

"Oh my God, Lisa, you have to. It feels so cool. You open your mouth and kind of suck on a boy's tongue."

"That's not the way it looks on TV."

"No, they don't do it right. It's different when you do it in real life. It's so much fun. I don't know why, but I like it."

"Have you kissed a lot of boys?"

"Yes, like ten. Maybe more."

"When? You're only fifteen."

"Well, the first time I was eleven, and then in the city, we used to play games and then have to go somewhere with a boy and do stuff."

"Like what?"

"I don't know. We would just dare each other to do stuff and then we would find a boy and do what the girls dared you to do."

"Did you want to?"

"Yeah, I wanted to. There was nothing else to do. I kind of liked being with the boys. It was fun."

"What else did you do besides kiss them?"

"I let them touch me without any clothes on."

"Where?"

"All over."

"Did you like it?"

"Sometimes it was weird, but it was okay. Sometimes they would dare me to give the boys a blowjob or to have them go to third base on me. That felt a little weird, but there was nothing else to do. And the boys in our group liked me. They always wanted to get with me. They said I was the prettiest. Which was cool. Nobody used to say that to me in school."

I should just leave, you know. All this stuff behind me. Just keep moving along. Walk right out into the horizon. All I would really need is just a couple of bucks in my pocket. It shouldn't be so hard to come by. I have a little bit saved, and maybe I could sell some of my shit. I should do that. I should just get the fuck out of here right now. When nobody's looking, I should just steer off with this horse of mine, head off in another direction. Or maybe I should just get that money, head out west somehow, hitchhike or some shit and buy my own horse. Maybe I could find some work out there on a farm or something and pay my own way. Not everybody graduates high school. My grandmother Jerry only finished up to the eighth grade, and her life was fine. I don't see why I need to go through all that bullshit. I shouldn't be forced to go through all that ugliness like that, and for what? So I can learn basic algebra and world fucking history. There ain't no shit they can teach me I can't learn myself in a book.

I like books anyway. I've read a lot of them, and I don't mean the stupid shit they make you read in school. There was this one book I loved. Read it a few times, even. It was about a group of guys that just lived however the fuck they wanted to, going from city to city, hustling for money. Life was trying to strangle the shit out of them, but they just said fuck it and set off for the horizon in some really cheap car, a jalopy I think they called it. That Jack Kerouac, he knew a lot about the good life. It's too bad he didn't live for that long. I think he knew that it was so shitty here, it wasn't worth sticking around. I only read that one book of his, but I sure would like to read more, figure out how he was able to be free like that.

I see Andrea up there ahead of me. Her long, brown ponytail keeps shifting from side to side. She's all the way up front, right behind the guide. She said she's never been on a horse before, but she picked it up right away. We all had to take time to bond with our horses, to feed them and comb their hair. We spent about a half hour doing that shit, which I thought would be kind of a drag, but I think I liked it instead.

Animals. I never do give them enough thought, but they are usually so gentle. Even the big ones that seem like they could be mean and cruel, all seem like little lost puppy dogs when you see them up close. I remember seeing these pictures of these black rhinos when I was a kid, and I thought they looked just brutal, like if you ever came anywhere near those things, they would rip you apart. But not too long ago, I was watching this special on PBS at like 2:00 in the morning, just on those rhinos, and you know, up close, they looked timid and docile, like they just wanted to play and drink and eat and do whatever it is they do on those plains out there in Africa. There used to be so many of them, all spread out almost infinitely across that whole continent, and now there's hardly any, like a couple hundred or some shit. People kill them, for stupid reasons, just to take their little horns and then just leave them there to die. That's the way of it. The vultures are always out, watching for a moment of weakness.

"Hey Lissahhhhh. How ya feeling? Seeing any *traaails* lately?" she says, coming up next to me on that horse of hers. I was really enjoying myself too. I had a nice little pocket of quiet for nearly forty minutes, and, thanks to my new BFF, I have a feeling it's abruptly coming to an end. "So how ya feeling, Chiquita? Enjoying your day? Feeling *reelaaaxed*?"

"Yeah, I'm fine, Allison." I get the feeling she's hinting about that little pill she gave me earlier. To be honest, I have been feeling a little relaxed, but I can't say I feel high or anything like that. It's mellow. I'm glad I took it.

"Don't worry, Lisa. I grabbed the key to the pharmie chest last night, so there's more where that came from, if you know what I mean." Then she gives me one of her infamous winks and rides off ahead of me to catch up with the guide.

"Hey, mister. What da ya say, you and me ride up ahead and do a little trotting. I've been riding since the fifth grade, so I'm really chill if you know what I mean."

"Sorry, honey," I hear him say to her. "We all have to stay together now, and since the other girls are inexperienced, we need to keep it slow."

"All right. I'm chill. I'll just hang back with my girls then, maybe show them a trick or two."

And I pray and pray that by "her girls" she doesn't mean me. I think I've had just about all I can handle for the day. This is

Dana's idea; I know it is. She's always trying to get us to do some group bonding bullshit. Normally, we have to break up into different factions when we're out and make friends with some of the other girls in other groups. Some of them live in our house. Some of them live in the hospital. I guess it depends on where you fall on the spectrum of mental health. When I first got here, they kept me in that hospital for two days, monitoring me for a full forty-eight hours to make sure I wasn't gonna break the window and slit my wrists with the glass or some shit. They had me on so many meds I didn't have any idea where I was to begin with.

But I have to say I like all of this. I don't mind being out here. The weather's been so crappy lately. Too much rain. Freezing, bitter rain. But every once in a while, the sun comes out, and you can hear the pleasant sound of birds returning, like the hermit thrush coming up from Central America; to me, they sound like little fairy flutes singing in the forest. When I listen to them, it's easy to pretend I'm somewhere else. That's what it's like today, and I just want to be calm and soak it in.

When we first got here, we had to sit and listen to our instructor give us this hour long rundown on how we should behave around a horse. A horse is really sensitive, he said. He knows if you fear him or if you trust him. He said, without trust, the horse will be very erratic. He'll get anxious and bothered when you ride him. But when you give that horse trust, he will care for you as if you are one of his own. He said a very special bond could develop between a horse and a person when they develop trust. And I look over at Andrea when he's saying all that and can see she's ready to run out and move to a horse farm or become a veterinarian or some shit just because the easy idea of love is so tempting for her.

I sit there and buy his bullshit too. Of course, I'm fully aware of the ulterior motive involved with all this horse bonding crap, but whatever. It's not with another person, so I say fuck it. I'll give it a try. I think about Dana and what she said to me before, how she arranged all this because she thought I would like it. And I wonder why she didn't come with the rest of us.

The Oak Room was located on South Martin Luther King Boulevard, a street Dana had to walk down for two miles each way, north and south, at four and at six, on Tuesday and Thursday evenings, from October to May, from the time she was eight until she was twelve, to get to St. Joseph's Church on the corner of Jefferson and Washington, as she prepared to make her final commitment to the Catholic Church. She always loved the month of September, when she could come home and just relax in front of the TV or play a game with a neighbor. But when October came, it was like going to double school with more homework twice a week. And the nuns who taught the religion classes were not like the teachers at her school who told stories and let the girls go out in the back to play if they finished their school work early. No, the nuns wore all black, and all their hair was tucked back under a habit, and their faces were always serious. Dana was afraid of them, all four of them, who taught all four years of after school classes until she made her confirmation.

When she was eleven, the year before the ceremony, she had to choose a saint to study, whose name she would adopt as her own middle name, and the only name that came to her mind was the only woman she wanted to know about besides her mother: her grandmother, Benedetta. A woman she had never known, whose arms had never held her, whose gentle hands had never touched her face, whose soft voice she never heard sing a soothing melody as Dana fell asleep as a baby, whose face she had only known from an old picture of her as a child standing next to her great-grandfather in a home-made embroidered communion dress. The picture was left on her Aunt Geraldine's doorstep the morning of her own communion three years earlier in a white box. Underneath the picture was an opal cross, looped around a gold chain small enough for a child's neck. There was no card or note that took credit for the gift, only a little inscription on the back of the picture that said, "from your mother."

Dana knew even before she opened the box. It had to be from her father. And she opened the box and put the cross around her neck and stared at the picture of her grandmother wearing the same cross, on the same day in her own life, a present from both her mother and her father, two people she always hungered to know, but knew she never would; she always prayed that one morning she would wake up and things would be different, that she would open her eyes and hear the voices of her own parents arguing over breakfast instead of Aunt Geraldine and Uncle Joseph. When she opened the box, she felt a part of something, instead of just the extra person her aunt and uncle had to take care of in a house that was too small for the children in their own family. She never felt unloved by them, and they never treated her any differently than their four other children who all treated Dana like a sister, but she knew that she didn't belong to them, that even though they were her family, they weren't her family, not the family Dana had wanted.

Twenty

I think I'm gonna grow my hair out really long. I think from now on, I'm gonna stop cutting it, and I'm just gonna let it grow as long as I can get it. Andrea has long hair. She wears it up a lot, in a bun mostly, but sometimes she lets it just hang down behind her back. Sometimes I look at her and feel jealous, especially when she lets her hair down like that. I'm jealous because I wish I looked pretty and innocent just like her and that I also had hair that fell gently and loosely behind my back.

Maybe I'll change the color too. Make it red like Sara's or put some blonde highlights in it to lighten up my face. I'll start dressing differently too. Get some dresses and some long flowing skirts and walk around barefoot like a hippie. I'm going to do all this when I go out west. Be a different person. I'm going to take a pen out and write a script tonight, yes, I'll do it tonight when the others are sleeping. I'll take a pen out, and I'll write out a script of my new life, of how I will look and how I'll be when I move out west, and I leave all this crap behind me, so far back that I can't even remember what any of it ever looked like to begin with.

"Lisa, Lisa," she says in a hurried voice. It's Amanda. "Did you have fun? I had fun. I just loved riding on the horse. I can't wait till tomorrow morning when we can do it again. Dana said I can only do it if I don't give her any trouble about dinner tonight. But I won't, I promise. I'll eat everything. I think I lost a few pounds last week anyway. I was able to get into these jeans this morning, and I haven't worn them in months. Don't I look good?" And she turns around so I can see how snuggly they fit around her ass, I presume.

I just smile and say, "Of course, Amanda. You look really good. Those jeans look great on you," but what I really should say is you look awful. It looks like a hefty gust of wind could come by and break you into pieces. If you sat on your ass and watched *Days of Our Lives* for the next three months, eating only hot dogs and donuts till you felt nauseous, you still wouldn't come close to looking like a normal human being. But I don't.

"Lisa, I ate my whole lunch today too. You saw me. I ate everything that was in that box, even the cookies. You'll tell her, right. I know you tell her things."

"Tell who, Amanda? I don't know what you're talking about."

"Dana, Lisa. I saw you talking to her before, and she gave you a list. I'm sure she asked you to keep an eye on us. And you'll go back and tell her everything. She trusts you. You're her favorite. I can tell."

Oh my God. It's a conspiracy. "Amanda. I don't know what you're talking about. She just told me to give out these stupid lunches and not to be late for dinner. I'm not gonna go back to her with a report or anything."

"But you'll tell her I ate my lunch, though? Won't you do that for me?" she begs, pulling me in closer to her. "Please, Lisa. You'll do that for me, won't you?" And I can tell something in her is panicked, like there's more to the story than just wanting to ride horses again in the morning. I guess now that I think about it, she was looking over at me incessantly before when we were sitting under that tree, eating those boxed lunches. She was looking at me like she was putting on a show, and I was the main audience.

"You'll tell her for me, won't you?" she repeats with an air of desperation.

"I'm not her little minion, Amanda, and I don't want anyone going around saying that I am. But yeah, I'll tell her. Because it means a lot to you, I'll do it."

And she looks over at me with a great big smile of relief like I just got her out of some major trouble with the school principal or some shit. Then she jumps up and wraps those bony little arms around my chest and holds on like she doesn't want to let go. "Thank you, Lisa. Thank you. Thank you. Thank you. Thank you."

"All right, all right, Amanda. No big deal," and I start to

peel those little arms away from me when I hear that annoying voice creeping up behind me.

"Hey ladies, watcha ya doin'? Hey ladies, watcha ya doin'? We're gonna take the cars out and go busting down the highway," she sings with some stupid offbeat rhythm to her voice.

"It's bussing through the street corners," I explain, though I feel a little sick to my stomach that I know the lyrics well enough to correct Allison.

"Whatever, bitch. I know. I just like busting down the highway better. So I put my own little spin on it. I got to get those creative juices flow'n in me from time to time. It's the only thing that keeps me half straight. You know what I mean, jelly bean?"

Oh wow. I think she's looking over at me for some type of response. And now I'm caught up in it again. It just never ends.

"Where did Andrea go? I thought she was with you. Dana's gonna blow a whistle if we're late."

"Would you just take those panties out of your ass, girl? She's over there in the barn flirting with the instructor. Let her have her fifteen minutes."

Her fifteen minutes. Whatever.

"Just let her get her kicks." Allison continues. "All we have to do is walk over to that restaurant. It can't be more than three minutes away. What'cha afraid that Dana's gonna give you a little demerit if we all walk in there at 6:02 or something? Don't worry, Lisa, you can blame it on the old troublemaker, write it down on that score card she gave you to monitor my behavior."

"I don't know what the fuck you're talking about, Allison, as usual."

"Sure you don't, Lisa."

"Whatever."

"Yeah, whatever."

"You got a fucking problem?" And I'm about to lose it on her and the fucking bullshit she's trying to insinuate here. And then suddenly I get the feeling she's throwing that shit around that I'm Dana's little lackey, running back to her with all my little tattletales on the other girls. Like that ain't the straw that broke the camel's back. That psychotic little bitch has been running around telling everyone that I'm a little nark. And just like she knows I'm gonna jump out of my skin, Amanda jumps in the middle of us and intercedes.

"Come on, guys. We have the whole cabin to ourselves tonight. Let's not ruin it by fighting."

"Hey, girl. No one's fighting. We're all just tripping here, aren't we, Lissaahhh?"

"Yep, tripping," I just comply, for whatever the fuck that's supposed to mean. After all, something's gotten into both Amanda and Andrea today. You know, maybe in myself as well. I think it's the fresh spring air. I think it's gotten all of us a little hopeful, probably a tad bit too optimistic, but what the fuck. I'll bite. Even if it's just for the day, I'd like to soak it up as much as I can.

"Hey, Amanda," she says, giving her what's supposed to be a private little wink, I presume. "I got something you would like right in my little pocket here."

"Allison, no," she says, shaking her head and bugging her eyes out, like she's afraid Allison's gonna reveal a dirty little secret right in front of me, the spy.

"Chill out, girl. Lisa's down, aren't you, Lisssaaahhh?"

If I see another one of those sly little winks of hers, I'm really gonna puke all over the place.

"Aren't you chill, Lisa? I got something else for you too if you're down?"

"All right. Let's just cut the innuendo bullshit. If you got something to give out, just pass it over. Enough with all the chit-chat."

"All right, Lissaaahhhh. Have it your way. But what da ya say we step it up a notch?" and she puts her hand in her pocket and puts three more little blue pills in my palm.

"So how chill are you, girl? Ready to get off a little?"

What the fuck. I just throw my head back and toss that shit in my mouth and swallow.

"Sorry Amanda, but Lisa just downed the rest of my shit. I didn't know she was so hardcore. I guess she's not all talk like I thought she was."

And all of a sudden, Amanda looks cold and sallow, the way you could imagine a junkie waiting on an abandoned street corner for a dealer who never shows up. And then it just hits me, all of a sudden like that, looking at her all scared and shaking at the thought that I swallowed all those pills that Allison brought with her. That's how she keeps it off. Even in here, where they're monitoring everything that she's eating and following her in the bathroom to make sure she doesn't puke it all up. Allison's been sneaking her those pills every night when she's going through that medicine chest. Pills that speed up her metabolism like a racehorse.

"Oh chill out, Amanda. You've been standing here talking to Lisa for too long. I've got plenty of that shit in my pocket to last us till that sun comes up in the morning."

Twenty-One

In the back of my mind, I see blue, peaceful baby blue. And the air feels soft and cool. There's a slight breeze rubbing against my cheek. I hear the gulls in the background with their high-pitched squeaking. Louder and softer. Louder and softer. Their voices cascade. I look up and see blue. Just blue. No white clouds. I've never seen anything so pristine. "Just close your eyes." That is the voice I keep hearing. "Just close your eyes and let go." And so I do. I close my eyes.

"Snap out of it, girl. Dana's looking over here, and she's gonna flip if she sees you spacing out like that. You'll get us all into trouble."

"What? Allison. I'm fine. I'm fine," I say, trying to get my eyes straight. "I just got distracted for a bit."

"Well, you better pull yourself together real quick because I see Dana in the corner over there with her eyes fixated on our table. Pull your shit together for five fucking minutes until I blow her off. Then I say we blow this Popsicle stand."

"Whatever. I'm fine."

Wow. I don't know where I was for a minute.

"Well, you better eat something. Both of you. You better not fuck things up for me tonight. I got my girl Colleen coming to meet us at that red barn in the back across the field, and she's bringing a liter of vodka. The good shit too. Not that generic fucking liquor store crap."

"Your friend's coming here? I don't think that's a good idea, Allison. If Dana catches us then we're all gonna be in trouble, and I'm already on the warning list."

"Chill out, Amanda. No one's gonna get fucking in trouble. Lights are out by ten pm sharp. That means everybody will be sound asleep by eleven. I guarantee you there ain't gonna be no guards out there monitoring us."

And I'd really like to know how Allison can be so sure none of us are gonna get caught sneaking across a field in the middle of the night, high off of God knows what and now seemingly a little drunk off of whatever premium vodka her friend has coming. I have to admit, question after question seems to be building up in my mind, but what seems to be taking center stage through all of this is the little comment that Amanda just mentioned.

"What do you mean, a warning list? I've never heard of a warning list before."

"Nothing, Lisa. Don't worry about it. Forget that I mentioned it."

And I think about doing just that seeing as I usually try to keep myself from butting into other people's beeswax like that, but a little smirk Allison had made over to Amanda when she passed that comment made my curiosity too overbearing.

"Yeah, I see what you're saying there, Amanda, and I sure would like to respect your privacy and all, but I just wonder if you could pass me a little hint about this whole warning list concept and what it perhaps entails."

"It's no fucking big deal. I've been written up so many times for so many fucking bullshit reasons in this place. She's just overreacting."

"She's right, Lisa. I'm just overreacting because she called my dad, and now we have to have some type of emergency meeting on Monday. I just don't want her to tell on me," she says, completely flushed, and she looks over at me and takes a heaping spoonful of sweet peas off her plate and puts them in her mouth with the greatest expression of disgust I think I've ever seen in a human being. Dinner time's almost over, and she's anxious to clear some of the food off her plate before Dana makes her mandatory stopover at our table to make sure we're keeping in line.

And I just can't hold it, so I have to ask, "What are you afraid she's gonna tell your father, Amanda? What could possibly be so bad?"

"Oh, nothing, Lisa. It's nothing, really," she says, pushing her fork to move uneaten food around her plate.

"Oh chill out, girl. Lisa's not gonna do anything." And Allison turns to look at me. "She's been puking in little plastic bottles and sneaking them out into the hallway trash in the middle of the night when those two jerk-off nurses are smoking a storm away downstairs, doing nothing. I bet you by the end of next week that will be the last we see of Jackie and Margot."

"Allison," Amanda says, more flushed than ever. "You promised you wouldn't tell."

"Oh, chill out. We're all sistas in this group of ours, aren't we? Aren't we supposed to be bonding on this little trip? Well, we can't very well do that if we keep all of our deep, dark secrets inside."

And I can tell Amanda is flush out of quick responses, so I just look over and jump in. "Well, that's an interesting way to look at things, Allison. Why don't we take a break from Amanda and start digging into your dirty little secret bag."

"I already unleashed it all in group. I don't have anything else to hide from you all. Poke around, Lisa, you won't find anything you're looking for."

"Yeah, well, if what you're saying about Jackie and Margot is correct, and they're about to get booted, what are you going to do about your sticky little fingers and your midnight habit of going into the medicine cabinet?"

"I'm chill, bitch. I'm just trying to help out some of the

sistas who need it. I ain't got no problem if that's what you're implying."

"Implying what, Allison, that you're a fucking junkie? They just pulled you in from the streets less than two months ago. The fucking heroin needle was still probably stuck in your arm."

"Oh, yeah, Lisa, well how *you* feeling?"

"I'm feeling fine."

"Oh, yeah, Lisa, how *you* feeling? I'm sure Dana would like to know how many oxies her Little Miss Goody Two-Shoes put in her mouth today."

"Be quiet," Andrea shouts from the corner of the table. She was sitting there keeping to herself, but now I can see those fingers are up in her mouth. "Dana can see you, and now she's heading over here."

"Oh my God. Oh my God. I didn't eat enough. Oh my God. Allison, help me."

"Chill out, girl. Slide me that piece of meat. I can swallow it whole before that bitch gets over here."

And she does. She takes that shit off of Amanda's plate and shoves it down that throat of hers before any of us have a chance to blink, and two-point-two seconds later, Dana's standing there to the left side of the table right next to Andrea, making her bite down on those fingernails even harder.

"How you guys doing over here? It looks like things were getting pretty heated for a bit. Everything all right?" And she looks with her eyes shifting between Allison and me to see if one of us will break and cough up and confess first. She's trying to break up those little glances evenly among the two of us, but I know she's itching for me to spill about some stupid shit that Allison is up to, but I can't give her or anyone else the satisfaction, so I just sit there with my arms crossed.

"It was nothing, Dana." It's Andrea again. For some reason, I think she's a little paranoid too about these warning lists that seem to be going around. She just looks up at Dana and comes up with this piece of bullshit. "They're just talking about Run DMC and Aerosmith and who really did 'Walk This Way' better. Honestly, I don't know what they're talking about and don't care. I just want to see the man speaking tonight in the auditorium. I wanted to be sure to get a good seat, so I can ask him some questions. Dana, would you walk over there with me?"

"That sounds like a great idea, Andrea. Why don't we all walk over there together?"

"Oh yeah, Andrea, that sounds like a *great* idea," Allison adds with a cunning little smile planted in her direction. "Oh, yeah, but Amanda was just saying that even though that wholesome, nutritious meal they just supplied us with was mighty fine, she sure would like to get her hands on a nice piece of that double chocolate tart they got over there on that dessert bar, weren't you saying that Amanda?"

And Amanda just moves her eyes around the table, unsure

of what to say all on her own. "Yes, Dana. If that's okay, I would like to stay and have some dessert tonight."

"Yes, of course, Amanda. I'm glad you have a bit of an appetite. The food here is a bit different than the hospital. What, perhaps, did you like better about it?"

And Amanda is stuck because she never really did much of her own eating tonight nor did she ever acquire the skills of being a good liar like her new BFF has collected over the years, so she just sits there and looks around with a little bit of a confused look on her face.

"It's the dessert she's been eyeing since we've gotten here this evening, isn't it Amanda? Hasn't tasted it, but it's the dessert she's holding on for as her favorite, ain't it Amanda?"

And Amanda just looks up with a brief smile of relief and says, "Sure is. I've been looking forward to having some chocolate all night."

"Well, nothing's wrong with that. I had a piece myself, and it was pretty good."

Amanda and Allison. Something's going on between the two of them. I just can't put my finger on it. I've never seen Allison so eager to jump up and defend someone as she has been with Amanda for the past couple of days, at least this is the first time I've noticed it.

"And what about you, Lisa? Still haven't gotten your appetite back? You barely touched your meal. You don't like steak anymore?"

And before I can say anything, Allison jumps in again. This time to seemingly defend me, for some reason.

"To be honest with you, Dana, I think Lisa's been contemplating this whole neo-vegetarian thing a little too seriously. In actuality, that was part of the heated debate the two of us were just engaged in. I was arguing in favor of the long standing tradition of carnivorous living amongst the human race, defending the choices of our ancestors to eat meat and all, even in environments where plant materials seem to have been abundant, and Lisa was leading us into this whole ethical conversation about where our food comes from and shit while I'm trying to sit here and enjoy the only good piece of flesh I've had in some time. Honestly, I think anyone might be a little upset under similar circumstances." And Dana looks over and shakes her head in agreement, looking perplexed like she always does when Allison opens her mouth and says something ridiculous. "But I did just hear her tell Amanda that she plans on accompanying her over to the dessert bar to indulge in some of those cakes they got going over there."

And Dana looks over at me to verify. "So you're feeling all right then, Lisa? You're still looking a little flush."

"I'm doing fine, Dana. It's just the sleep thing from last night, like I was saying before. A little sugar will do me good."

"All right. Then why don't you eat your dessert and go

back to the room and lie down for the night. Maybe by tomorrow you'll have some more energy."

"And I'll make sure she gets there just fine. I think I'm gonna take it easy myself tonight."

"And you, Amanda?"

"I think I'll just head back with them, Dana, if that's okay? I would like to get some rest before we go on the horses again."

"Well, you'll be missing the speaker, but if you're okay with it, I'm sure Andrea could fill you in a bit in the morning. All right, then I'll say goodnight." And Dana and Andrea start to make their exit when Dana holds back and pulls one of her trademark one more things. "Oh, Lisa," she says, rubbing her ear like she has something smart aleck to say. "What time are we going to meet here for breakfast in the morning?"

"Seven am sharp, Dana. I remember."

"And I'll be sure to make sure she's here," Allison has to add. "You can count on that."

"All right. Then I'll say goodnight for real. Get some rest." And finally she walks away towards the door.

"Oh Lisa, you fucking rock. Toss me a high five." But I just stare at her gesturing over her head like a moron. "Come on. Don't be shy."

"Cut the crap, Allison. People are looking."

"Whatever. Who gives two shits? You just bought us all a free ticket out of a bullshit ex-drug addict discussion that we're supposed to all sit around and cry over for the next hour and a half. I wonder why Andrea was so eager to get in there like that?"

"You know why, Allison," says Amanda. "Andrea likes those inspirational speakers. She always thinks one of them is gonna lead her to the answers she's been looking for."

"Yeah, whatever. As long as she keeps that Holy Bible bullshit away from me. Whatever floats your boat. That's what my homegirl Kelley used to say. Hey, what da ya say, Amanda, we go put on a show and raid that Viennese table they got going over there? We'll take a couple of pieces, and I'll slide them down for the both of us. No problem."

"You go on ahead. I'll catch up in a second," I say. "Just gonna finish some of these greens before dessert."

But the real reason is, all of a sudden, I'm feeling a bit hot and clammy. I'm glad Allison and Amanda have gone off and left me for a few minutes. I don't know what's wrong. Just a couple of deep breaths, and I should be okay.

God, the food is really gross. A plate full of bleeding meat and mushy frozen vegetables. And it's so loud. There are too many voices bouncing all around the room, vibrating through the cold, cement blocks. Too many sensations coming at me at once. I feel dizzy. I feel sick. I feel like I'm gonna black out.

The hunters,

The archers,

Are adept

At throwing their darts

To hit the target,

With their keen eye.

Their throw is

Sharp,

Smooth,

Centered.

They hit,

Straight on.

You,

The isolated board

On the bare wall,

The bull's eye,

The red dot.

Twenty-Two

"Lisa, they were just two people."

"No, they were everywhere. "

"What did they do to you? You have to tell me."

"I can't go back there."

"Yes, you can, Lisa."

"Paul did everything he could to get into the popular crowd. He would tell jokes in class and make himself the center of attention. And it worked. Everybody liked him.

"At first, he didn't even know who I was. And he didn't talk to me. But then, he started noticing the way other people treated me. How they would leave me out of things. And so he started getting in on it. And it was worse than the others. He would tell jokes about me in class, so everybody could hear. And sometimes he would throw notes at me that would call me ugly, and other people would see, and they would laugh. I swear, he made everybody hate me."

"And what about Josh?"

"I used to like Josh when I was in junior high. Other people knew. He knew it too, but it was never a big deal."

"And then what happened?"

"Paul found out. And him and Josh became friends, and he used to make Josh say things to me."

"Like what, Lisa?"

"Like make fun of me to my face about how I used to like him, and then they would laugh at me, like it was a joke. And I couldn't get away from them. Sometimes, if I tried to walk away, they would stop me. Like if I tried to walk away from them in the commons, they would corner me as best they could, so I couldn't leave. I had to stand there and listen to them make fun of me until I started crying."

"So, they would physically harass you too, Lisa? Is that what you're saying?"

"I don't know. I mean, I guess they would sometimes."

"Lisa, how many times did they put their hands on you?"

"I don't know how many times. I don't know. I just felt like I couldn't get away from them."

"Lisa, tell me what happened that day."

"Don't make me do that."

"You have to tell me what happened."

"It's my fault. I cut class so I could leave and go smoke. We were playing volleyball. I hated gym so much."

"Where did you go?"

"I walked to the back of the school grounds. If you walk all the way to the back, there are old tunnels. The security never goes back that far, so sometimes, when kids cut, they go down there to hang out. But not many kids know about it. I've never seen anybody down there before, when I was alone."

"And what happened when you got there?"

"I thought I was by myself."

"But you weren't?"

"No. They were there. I couldn't see them at first. They came out of nowhere. Josh and Paul. Out of all the people in the whole school that could be there, it had to be them. And I could see it in their eyes when they came towards me. They weren't gonna leave me alone."

"What did they say, Lisa?"

"It was Paul. He said that Josh really liked me. He was just saying that he didn't. And all this time he wanted to get with me."

"And then what else, Lisa?"

"And Josh said, yes, that was true. That he always had a crush on me. And that he always wanted to sleep with me. And that he wanted to do it then and that he wanted Paul to watch."

"And what did you say, Lisa?"

"I was scared. I didn't say anything. And I couldn't move. They just started getting so close to me. The both of them."

"How, Lisa?"

"I don't know. I could just feel them all over me. All over

me. And I can still feel what their bodies felt like. They were hot. And they put their hands on my arms. Both of them. They wouldn't let me move. I didn't want them to do that."

"I know, Lisa."

"But they wouldn't leave me alone. They trapped me, like they always did before, so I couldn't leave."

"Hey, look who it is."

"You down here all by yourself?"

"Of course she's by herself. She doesn't have any friends."

"But she has you, Josh. Aren't you her friend?"

"Oh, yeah, she has me. Maybe she'll do something for me, now that we're down here alone."

Lisa doesn't speak. She doesn't know what to do. She just watches, their amusement growing as the fear inside of her becomes more apparent.

"You gonna show Josh how much you like him now? I could leave you two alone." Paul smiles through the left side of his mouth and moves closer to Lisa. She can feel the heat from his body and his slight erection as he rubs up behind her.

Lisa's body is still, but her skin is starting to warm as the fear gets more intense.

"Come on, Lisa. You gonna show Josh how much you like him? Come on, Josh. Lisa's ready to show you, aren't you, Lisa? This is your chance."

Josh, hesitantly at first, moves closer.

"Is that what you want to do? Do you want to show me?"

Lisa, wrapped tightly between them, is too shaken to recognize what is happening; she can feel the warm, sweaty heat from their bodies, moving and rubbing into her.

Josh's mouth shifts to the left side of her face. His sweat drips on her skin. "Come on, Lisa."

She can feel the rhythm of his body as he rubs himself up and down. Paul is behind her.

The shock, then, wears off. She is covered with their moist heat and can feel warm, humid air coming from both of their mouths.

Fear takes over.

"No," she says as she begins to react, but only quietly. She is afraid to move, unsure of what they will do. "No," she says again and tries to shake herself away.

But they don't let her go.

"Finally, I pushed myself away and just ran. Dana, I didn't want them to do that."

"I know you didn't."

"I can always smell them and hear them and feel them, always, even when I'm asleep. I don't know what to do to make them go away."

"Is that why you tried to kill yourself, Lisa? So you could get away from them?"

"I can't do it. I know that they're out there. I know when I leave."

"What Lisa?"

"They'll find me. There's no way to escape all the people of my past."

"What if there was?"

"But there's not. It's not real."

"But what if there was, Lisa? What if you could make them go away? What if you never see them again?"

"They'll find a way to find me, even at St. Pat's."

"Lisa, I don't think they will. You know, I live in a town twenty minutes from where I went to high school, and my family still lives in the same place, in the same house that I grew up in, and you know what Lisa, except for maybe one or two people, I've never seen anyone, except my friends, that I went to high school with. People don't just run into each other. They don't. I didn't really like my high school either. And I also didn't have that many friends. But I never saw any of them. People forget really easily. They won't come looking for you. I know they won't."

"I don't know, Dana."

When she got older, she started going to that bar on South Martin Luther King Boulevard, although she became the only regular under fifty; but the men who thought of it as their second home didn't seem to mind. In fact, they kind of enjoyed having a woman around, especially one that was young and pretty and liked to listen to their war stories so much that she would usually spark up a conversation at the bar with, "So tell me that time when..." and they would all rush to fill in the blank at the end of her sentence before Dana had a chance to pause, so she never let on that she couldn't finish it on her own. Her basic knowledge of Vietnam soldiers came from college lectures and novels she took out of the public library that always had a heavy fictional spin to them, so much that Dana felt they could only offer weak images of the men who served there. Dana never felt satisfied learning about the war through pages of books written in voices she could never really hear. So just before she got old enough to order a drink for herself, she started going to the Oak Room and ordering Diet Cokes. But the bartender and the other men weren't satisfied with a person staking claim in their turf and not sharing at least one glass with hard liquor in it, so on Dana's second visit, the bartender Ralphie said that if she intended to hang there, she needed to at least have a single drink to sulk over, so he fixed her a Tom Collins, at no charge, never asking for ID to verify if she was even of legal age to be in the bar in the first place.

They never questioned why she was there, or why, as time

went on, she spent more and more of her weekend nights with a bar full of men that were old enough to be her father, who were all tired and out of shape from spending twenty-five years of life laying brick or putting up walls in high-rise buildings and spending their lunch hours in local bars drinking cheap beer. They just figured she was the awkward loner type, even though she was obviously intelligent and moderately beautiful. And they spent too many years dedicated to drinking heavy amounts of alcohol to ever intuitively question why she was so interested in hearing their stories from the war, particularly the really horror-stricken ones of the men they watched die in Vietnam and especially of the men who suffered afterwards.

She tried to block him out of her life; after all, he was a man she had no memories of being with and never came around to see her for the eight years of her life when he was alive. She knew a man who took care of her, whose house she slept in, who came to her dance recitals and sent her twenty dollar bills in little envelopes when she was just starting college and was living off of peanut butter and jelly and canned tuna fish. Uncle Joe, she called him, but she never called him dad, and even if she did, she would always know in her heart that it wasn't true, that her real father abandoned her when she was a baby and never responded to any of her letters pleading with him to come see her. Why, she asked God, why doesn't my father love me?

"Lisa, Lisa. Get up. We're supposed to be at breakfast soon." It's Amanda. She's shaking me. She keeps saying my name, over and over.

"Lisa, Lisa." I hear, as if I'm lost in a dark tunnel and there's an echo of a voice calling for me. "Get up. Get up. Or Dana's gonna know something's the matter."

"Where are we?" I say, trying to make sense of the hazy confusion that's my current state of mind.

"We're at the horse farm. Lisa, are you okay?"

"Yeah, I'm okay," I tell her. Then I sit up, and it hits me all at once. "Oh, but I feel like shit. What happened last night?"

It looks like a gigantic light bulb exploded in this room, my head vibrating in waves of dark and light.

"You really don't remember anything?"

And I go back and back, but I'm drawing a blank. Oh shit. I remember puking outside the barn. And Amanda holding my hair. I was taking shots of vodka and some other shit that tasted awful with Allison and that friend of hers.

"I remember getting sick. I feel like I was puking for hours. Oh, God. I think I even passed out in my throw-up. Did that really happen?" And I put my hand back to feel around for dried up puke spots in my hair.

"It scared me, Lisa. It was getting so late, and I didn't know what to do. I couldn't get you up. I came back and got Andrea, and she helped me carry you back here. Do you remember any of that?"

"Not really. Where's Andrea?" I say as I look around the room.

"She already left, Lisa. I think she's freaked out. Lisa, you were hallucinating. You thought I was your mother. You kept saying, 'Mom, Mom, why did you leave me?' I didn't know what to do. Andrea wanted us to call Dana, to take you to the hospital, to get your stomach pumped or something."

Holy shit. I don't remember any of this. What did I fucking do last night? The last thing I remember is sitting in that cafeteria, talking about chocolate cake with Dana. Now I have to get up and go horseback riding again. I don't think I can face everybody out there today, especially Dana.

"Oh my God, Amanda. What am I going to do? I can't even see clearly when I open my eyes."

"You have to get up and take a shower, Lisa. You got throw up all over your hair and your clothes. I didn't know what to do, so I threw them away in the dumpster in the back of the kitchen."

"You threw away my clothes?"

"Yes, Lisa. I didn't know what to do. It was Andrea's idea. She said there was no way you could clean all of that by the time we left, and we'd all get into trouble big time if Dana found out. Lisa, I can't have anything else smelling like throw-up. She'll think it was me. She'll know it was me. And I've already been warned once. Lisa, please get up and take a shower. Lisa, *please*. Before we get into trouble for being late for breakfast."

"All right, all right," I say. "I'll get up," and I do even though everything in my body wants to puke up anything that may be left in my stomach. I can't believe I got myself into this mess. That fucking bitch. I knew she was gonna get me into trouble.

And I finally gather what little energy I have to get up and look around the room even though that light is stinging through me like a squeeze of lemon juice on a flesh wound. And as I stretch my arms above my head and start to scan my eyes around, I notice there's a bed in here that hasn't been slept in.

"Where the fuck is Allison, Amanda?"

And she just looks down like she's trying to avoid telling me something I'm obviously gonna find out about. "I don't know, Lisa," she says, chomping on her fingernails. "Andrea went to go find her. Lisa, we only have one hour before breakfast. If Allison doesn't show up, Dana's gonna find out everything. And we'll all get kicked out. I can't go home, Lisa, not now. I'm not ready. Even all of this is too much for me to handle."

God, I wish I could remember something. The only memory that's playing over in my mind is throwing up in that dried up grass that pinched my skin. Amanda looks so freaked. And the strange thing is, to creep me out even more, it's as if I hear a string of police cars and fire trucks streaming through the background outside. I'm sure I'm just delirious, or it's just a coincidence or some shit. Anyway. Whatever. It will be fine. I'll just take a shower and feel better and pull myself together. Andrea will find Allison. She probably just passed out in the barn. I know any second now they'll both come walking through that door. And I look over at Amanda, and she's huffing and puffing like I've never seen anybody overreacting before.

"It's okay, Amanda," I say. "We have over an hour. Everything is going to be okay. What's the worse that could happen? Allison doesn't show up? She's the one that's gonna get into trouble. Dana would never know that we were all together," I tell her, even though I know I was supposed to be "watching her," though I would never admit I took on that responsibility.

"I don't know, Lisa," she says with her head all bopping around the room like she's got a million different scenarios building up inside of her and shit, like everything's all gonna fall apart, and she's gonna get kicked out and be forced to go home before she's ready, like she said before. Ready for what, I wonder?

And then Andrea walks through the door, and I start to feel a sense of relief, and I'm about to turn to Amanda and say, "See, I told you so. I told you everything was gonna be all right," when I notice that she's alone. And I wait to see if Allison's gonna come pulling up behind her with some stupid shit to say about what she did last night and why she got held up like she did, but that never does happen. It's just Andrea looking all scared and flustered and just standing there all quiet and shaking her head at us like she's talking in mime or some shit, saying, "Oh my God, we're fucked, we're fucked."

"Lisa, I want you to think about pressing charges."

"What?"

"Against Josh and Paul, for what they did to you."

"No."

"Lisa, you have to at least consider it. If they sexually assaulted you, they can't just get away with it."

"What do you expect me to do? Go to a police station? Go through a trial so everybody knows? No. I can't do that."

"Is it better then that you let them get away with it? Lisa, what if they do it to somebody else? They have to be held accountable for their actions."

"I can't do it. I can't go through all of that. I have to just block it out and get over it."

"Lisa, do you really think that's possible? Do you think you could just get over something like that and forget about it? It won't happen. It will never go away until you find some type of resolution. Lisa, I think that will come by holding them accountable."

"No. I can't. I won't do it. This is such a nightmare. I just want it to go away. Why can't you just leave me alone and let me forget."

"Lisa, like Allison did? Like she forgot? Is that what you want? Do you want to be like her? Because that's what she did, and it didn't work very well, did it?"

When Allison was ten, her mother's sister's daughter Angelina, who was sixteen years older than her, had two baby daughters of her own, but only the memory of a dead husband who left their home on a Friday night to go out drinking with his best friend, whose face Angelina would only see again through the gray skin and ghostly look of a corpse recently stitched up whole again in the basement of Schuler and Son's Funeral Home in the East Bronx.

There was nobody at fault. A man who was too old to be out walking by himself walked off the sidewalk when the light in the other direction was still green, and the man who was approaching the intersection was scanning the channels of the radio.

This is how Adam came into Allison's life.

After a year and a half, Angelina couldn't take looking at the fading yellow walls that needed painting or listening to the nagging cry of two little girls she couldn't care for with a wallet only filled with loose little pennies, so when she met Michael, a malpractice attorney who had just won a case, who owned a house with too many bedrooms and a yard so big that children could get lost in it, the fact that he had four children of his own, all who had mothers who had never been his wife, and a woman who the children once knew as their mother who had picked up and left after signing a divorce paper too many years ago for the children to remember, did not matter to Angelina. Too many children in a house she did not know. No, now all she thought of was a house that would keep her warm at night and a refrigerator filled with food that would keep *the stomachs of her two little girls filled at all times of the day.*

Allison's family welcomed Michael's family and very quickly thought of his children, though seemingly looking different on the outside, very similar on the inside, and the six children very quickly became brothers and sisters, nieces and nephews, cousins and stepchildren, big and small.

Allison remembers a time when they were all happy the night of Angelina and Michael's wedding. The kids slept over and stayed up all night while the honeymooners were preoccupied in a bedroom too far away for them to hear what was going on in the basement. The children—Adam, Tierney, Marissa, and Gerald, Krissy and Amy, Allison and Nicholas—all did their best not to interrupt the newly married couple.

They did kid stuff. Had contests over who could gargle the most water, played tag in the dark, told urban legend stories before they went to bed.

Allison remembers how Nicholas had always wanted a brother. He took to following Adam like a lost little sibling. It made her happy to see her older brother that way.

The girls that night had their own fun and told secret stories of boys they kissed in school closets when teachers weren't looking. They compared what it felt like—tongue or just sticky lips—on each other. This was, of course, when the boys weren't watching.

They were happy, making themselves sick on too many pieces of leftover wedding cake and getting high off of childhood imaginations, thinking of life that would be sweet with pink sugar frosting, and at the top of their own cake would be a man who could kiss better than any of the five of them. He would be handsome and tough and like to smoke, and, of course, would come home at night and make sure that she was happy. In their young thoughts, the lives ahead of them, all filled with adventure and men and fun little nights out, would be perfect, and they fell asleep excited about living it.

It was like that for a while, at least for a year and a half. All the cousins would get together, have sleepovers, laugh and be silly. So that, very quickly, they all seemed to blend together, and the family forgot that there was ever a time when Michael and the children were not part of their lives.

Then Allison was as pretty as a picture everybody wanted to hang on their walls.

That night, there was a half empty bottle of Grey Goose vodka laying on the empty floor in front of the dying flames of the fireplace in the basement of Michael and Angelina's house where Allison was sleeping on an old couch with no pull-out bed on the Saturday night of Thanksgiving break when she was thirteen.

That night, Allison fell asleep next to a fireplace with too many burning logs but woke up in a perverse dream that was so real she couldn't escape from it. Adam, lying on top of her, sweaty and smelling of vodka. She didn't know it would feel like that. Even when she dreamed about it being good, she didn't know it would feel like that. She woke up, and he was already inside of her. Her pants were already off. And before she could understand what was happening, before her thoughts could come into focus, he was done, and he just got up and left. All he left was the vodka, in front of the fireplace, that was barely lit anyway.

All night long, Allison looked at that half empty bottle, not sure what else to think. Until she picked it up and drank it, drank a half bottle of vodka, in a few gentle gulps. Then she felt sick. Then her stomach began to hurt and cramp. Then she knew what death would feel like, and she wanted it. She wanted it to come from that point on, so anything that could kill her became her closest friend. Her only friend. The only thing that knew about that night with Adam. Until she told a friend at school and that friend told everybody else. And everybody else was so loud about it, a school therapist found out and told her mother and the three of them all came together, once, for a meeting. And that was it. That was the only time Allison ever told and that was the only time her mother ever asked. It never came out again and her mother Catherine never said anything to her sister Jeanette and so Jeanette never said anything to her daughter Angelina who never said anything to her own daughters. It was hidden away, far down inside of Allison and blocked out and shielded away from her mother.

So Catherine never said anything as she watched the picture of her daughter grow ugly and distorted, skinny and frail, without sleep and without friends, wasting away. And that's how they kept it. One on the inside and one on the outside until the only thing Allison could think of was locking herself inside of a heroin vial, so she put a few T-shirts and a pair of jeans into a bag and ran away to Tristan, who had a never-ending supply and, for some reason she could never understand, wanted her around.

It's 6:55. I've showered, and everything looks neat and organized in our room, and we've all made sure that there's no evidence of anything. And I've super washed my hair and rinsed my mouth out with some heavy-duty mouthwash that Amanda carries around with a mint flavor that's so strong and so pungent it left a burning sensation in my mouth.

So all of us came back here and fell asleep, and that's all it was and all it looks like. Dana will never know about my missing clothes. I've brought plenty to spare. The only problem is Allison never did show up, and those ambulances I thought were part of my hung-over delirium got loud to the point that all of us could hear, and there's no mistaking that something's going on over there in the back of the woods, not too far away from that barn that we were hanging out in last night.

It's nothing. It's nothing. It's just a coincidence, I tell myself, though I'd have to be a really good liar to make myself believe it. We just sit there, all of us, on two parallel beds, made up of course, but left a little ragged, seemingly looking like they've all been slept in, without suspicion.

No one has any words, but sounds are still bouncing around the room. Creepy, ominous sounds. Foreboding sounds. Sounds you wish you could turn off or wake up from.

6:57. It's too late. We have to go over to the cafeteria and explain to Dana why Allison's not with us. And I'm about to open my mouth and gather everyone to get up and start moving, when who-do-you-know walks through the door, all bright-eyed and looking cheery and, best of all, like she ain't been through nothing but a good's night sleep, and she's ready to go start the day with a burst of adrenaline. And I don't even want to know. I'm just so relieved to see her; I pick up my shit and burn out the door before I even give her a millisecond to open up that stupid mouth of hers and give out some stupid bullshit reason about where she was and why she was late and why the fuck we spent all morning freaking out and looking all over for her when obviously there was nothing going on to begin with.

For some reason, I couldn't defend myself. I wish I had. I remember seeing this movie a few months ago, and these kids were sitting in a circle in class for some reason, and this one kid was saying something mean to this other kid, so that kid, he just got up and walked clear across that circle and punched him in the face. He must not have even been seven years old, and he was strong enough to defend himself. I remember when I saw that, I was jealous. I wished I could turn back the clock, so I could do the same. I mean, why did I just take it? I could have done something to fight back. There was no reason why I couldn't. But I just let them keep coming after me. I just sat there and cried and cried like a baby. I'm so mad at myself for that. There's a big part of me that I can't forgive.

Twenty-Three

The rest of the day was like a nightmare, and I'm so glad the only parts that are left involve me going back to my room and picking up my crap and going back to that bus to pass out for two hours on the way back to the hospital. I never did have many experiences with drugs and alcohol save a couple of puffs of marijuana throughout the day, and I can tell you now, as tempting as it sounded before to block away my troubles through the foggy disposition of a drug user, this little twenty-four-hour experience was just about all that I could handle, and it doesn't make me want to go running out to the street corner to get more. No wonder why Allison's so fucked up. Anyone who would want to feel like this on a regular basis has truly lost their mind.

I don't know what I was thinking taking all those pills yesterday. And the memories are all still kind of blank inside my head. I remember the inside of that barn. I can sort of piece it together in broken images. I remember the old, rusty pieces of barn equipment that looked like they had been locked up since the nineteenth century, and the straw we were all sitting on that was scratching my legs. And Allison's friend. She was a little girl. I mean, not in age or anything. In terms of that, I think she might have been older than us even cause she did have a car and all, but she was very small. I bet you she couldn't be more than five feet tall, maybe even 4'10" or some shit like that. I wouldn't be surprised if she was that short. And I bet you she must have weighed about ninety-five pounds or something, not emaciated like Amanda, but just small, you know. Anyway, she really didn't talk much, but she could throw that alcohol back like I never saw anyone do. For such a small girl, she seemed to hold it together fine. The last thing I remember before I ran outside to puke for the fifth time was her and Allison arm-wrestling on this old, wooden table that was barely held together. They went at it over and over again, each time Colleen beating the crap out of Allison, and each time Allison crying that she wanted a re-do because something seemed like it just wasn't right. Allison's always got to throw in some bullshit reason whenever things turn out where she's not on top. Anyway, that Colleen, she seemed like a nice girl, but I get the feeling she is way fucked up, just like Allison. Birds of a feather, I guess.

So Allison was trying to throw her line of bullshit at me all throughout the day, but I just couldn't take it. For the first time since I met her, I was bold and stood my ground. I just kept walking clear away from her, mid-sentence and everything, every time she'd open that stupid mouth of hers. Of course, she never does take the hint, so she goes on and on whenever she feels like she can corner you, but I just blatantly walked away every time she'd try to throw that bullshit at me.

It's not worth it. That's the only thing I've learned during my bullshit time here. None of this is worth it. For so many years now, I've thought about giving up my whole life because of other people, and for the first time, I feel like such a fool for all of that. I feel like such a fool because they're the ones that suck. Why should I sacrifice myself for them? For all the miserable bullshit I went through being on this farm for two days, there was the sun out and the trees opening up and coming back to life and all the land that seems to go on forever, land like I've never seen before, so much of it. I walk through it now, all by myself, to go back and get my bag, a little bit earlier than the others, so I can get on the bus and get a back seat and put my head down before everybody else piles on. I look over through everything out there, with all of them, all the others, all the people behind me, and I just look over at the horizon, at the sun going down and all the different colors in the sky, purples and magentas and blues and wavy patterns of puffy clouds. I look over and feel all the energy from God and know what I have to do. I'm going to go out west somehow. And I'm not gonna finish school. I'm just gonna gather what I can and go out there all by myself. Somehow, I'll pull it all together. Because the only thing I ever hated so much was all the bullshit from all the people around me. When I finally remove that layer, I know what's underneath could be just fine. I know that's where the hope could lie.

After I grab my bag and head to the bus, I turn around to soak it up as much as I can for the very last time. For the last time I'm out here in infinite space, coddled within the endless beauty of the mountains, for the last time before I make my move. I look around, and I breathe in deeply. I look at the colors blending into the falling sun. I hear the faint whispers of the bumpy wind and the echoes of the birds in the bordering trees. I feel whole for the first time and know this feeling will carry me through all the bullshit I need to go through in the upcoming weeks to get out of the hospital. I take one more deep breath and hold it in the bottom of my gut like we learned in yoga. This time with my eyes tightly closed. Then I release. I release all the crap and bullshit that's been loaded on top of me from other people. I release and send it away from me. Very far away.

Then I get to the bus and go all the way to the back. The last seat in the back corner by the window. I throw my bag on the shelf, bunch my knees up to the seat in front of me, and lay my head back. All I need is about ten minutes, and I can just blank out for the rest of the trip. I'll never even know when the rest of the crowd gets on-board this stupid bus.

All I need is just a few more weeks, I tell myself. Just a few more weeks, and I'll make a plan, and I'll get the fuck out of here.

And I won't tell no one where I'm going. And I close my eyes thinking of that place.

But, of course, the way life has it, it's never that easy. I close my eyes, but all I hear every thirty seconds is buzz, buzz, like someone left their stupid cell phone on vibrate. I try to ignore it and concentrate on this beautiful image I have in my head of the mountains out west, in the desert, like Arizona. I imagine the sun falling behind the landscape and the red sky, burnt brick red. I'm still on top of those mountains. There's a hawk circling below me, looking for prey. I close my eyes, and the hot desert air is warming my skin, even at sunset.

But every time I drift off into this quiet meditation, I am brought back to this stinging reality with the nuisance of that annoying buzzing sound that just won't relent. I know my only chance of falling deep into a dream state is if I cut off that sound for good, so I get up and follow that buzzing vibration all the way to the front of the bus where the driver must have left her bag. I know I shouldn't go through it and all, but I feel as if life has left me no other choice, and seeing as my very sanity is on the line, not to mention that I haven't had any real sleep in about forty-eight hours, I start digging through that purse of hers to look for that cell phone.

It's not really a phone after all. It's one of those brand new, state-of-the-art iPads they just released that probably costs five hundred dollars. I guess they pay these bus drivers more than I thought they did. She's got this thing set to some type of alert. I play with a few buttons and finally get the screen to light up. We're not allowed to have anything like this around. In fact, it's been months since I've held any type of computer device in my hands. It feels nice. I miss being able to surf the web. Not like do bullshit things like post stupid crap about the last time I picked my nose on Facebook, but I miss doing cool things like reading interesting facts about new birds I want to learn about, or just for shits and giggles, looking up interesting crap about cool places in the world I thought could be interesting to live. I'm tempted to spend my ten minutes of alone time playing with this little iPad of hers, but I'm too well positioned in my moment of Zen to stay distracted by a silly little thing like this, so I just fool around with it enough to figure out how to turn the stupid vibrator off.

She has it on some type of Yahoo! News alert, probably so she can know instantly the moment Kim Kardashian changes her nail appointment. I honestly can't figure out how to make this buzzing stop. It's still going on every thirty seconds, even in my hand. Then something pops up on the screen. This must be one of the alerts she was looking for:

Seventeen-year-old girl found dead in West Milford, discovered by jogger at 5:00 am this morning, apparently a drinking and driving accident. Police refuse to release her name, being it's a minor. We just have some details regarding her appearance. Brown hair. Ninety-seven pounds. 4'11" in height. Police say the accident probably happened at 4:30 am, shortly before the jogger stumbled upon the wreck and the girl's dead body. Preliminary test results reveal the girl's blood alcohol content was four times the legal limit. The body was found less than a mile away from Bryant Lake Horse Farm.

There is a calm in the midst of a storm, when things get quiet and the rays of the sun even become visible for a brief moment. The eye, I hear them call it, like God is breaking through the winds and the gray weather, opening up the heavens, offering us a brief moment of restitution. And a part of us believes that it's for real, and we fall back and release and let go with a brief sigh of relief, thinking, perhaps, that we have made it, safely over to another side where there are things that we had never imagined.

It was warm that day, so I went out without a jacket. I hadn't seen the sun for so long, and Sara convinced me it was time to go outside. She was right. I was closed up for too many weeks; taking a brief stroll outside the closed doors was more of a relief than I ever remembered was possible--to be with another, to touch another, to take another by the hand, and to trust that she would not let go of it, not for a long time, until I was ready to walk away on my own.

"I think Dana is an orphan," she said.

"Why would you think that?"

"Because I asked her once about the cross she always wears. She said it was a gift from her mother, but that she never met her. She said her father left it for her on the morning of her communion when she was eight-years-old. I didn't know what a communion was. She said it was something that Catholic people do when they are children."

"I had to do that too. It was all stupid. I had to go to these classes until I was thirteen. And then we had to go through this ridiculous ceremony and promise all these bullshit things, and then it was over. I haven't been to a church since. It was all just for show. Or something my mother did to relieve her conscience.

"That picture of that man on her desk in the army uniform, that's her father, isn't it?"

"I think so, but I didn't ask. I didn't think she wanted to talk about her mother too much, so I just dropped it."

"Yeah, she does that, Dana. We have to go on and on about us all the time, but she never wants to let us know about her. It's so hypocritical."

"I guess, Lisa. But she's okay. She doesn't bother me as much as she bothers you."

"She doesn't bother me, Sara. I just hate the way she keeps on top of you all the time. Sometimes, I just want her to back off and leave me alone."

"Me too, I guess. But I think that's why she pushes us so much. She wants us to have what she never did. She never had a chance to be with her family, so I think it will make her feel better if we do. I don't know. My mother hasn't even come here yet."

"Do you like your mother?"

"She usually leaves me to myself, and I like that. I just wish she would have asked me a few times about what I wanted."

"It's strange. They just don't seem to think about us at all, do they? I wonder, sometimes, why they even had us to begin with."

"Because babies make people think about God, don't you think, Lisa, 'cause they look so beautiful and all? And everybody wants to be close to God."

"I don't know, Sara. I never thought about it like that."

"In the middle of third grade, we did something else I didn't want to do. We moved to the city, to Jersey City, right outside of Manhattan. My mother used to take me down to the river to look across the water at those big buildings. I think she was trying to be nice or something. But it scared me. I'd never seen anything like it. Out west, we lived in the desert. To me, New York was like living on another planet. I was afraid of all those people and the sound of all the sirens that seemed never-ending.

"But one day, when I was in my room, I was just lying on my bed and all, and I heard this sound, like a whistle, coming from outside. Like it was something on the roof.

"That sound, it would come and go. Most of the time, I just thought I was crazy. But I always felt like, when I really wanted to try to make it all go away, you know Lisa, it was there outside my window singing, wanting me to hear it.

"One day, when I was waiting outside for the bus with my mother, I looked up at the sky, and it was there, sitting on the roof of my building. A monk parakeet with soft green and blue feathers, just sitting on the ledge. I swear it was looking directly at me, right into my eyes. This beautiful green parakeet. I never knew those things could come all the way up here. I just remember seeing them on TV once. And knowing that they lived down south, all the way down, like by the equator.

"I remember when I saw those birds on that show, one of those specials that come on late at night; there were toucans and other birds that I never knew about before, like pink flamingos, and some others that I can't remember right now.

"I remember that feeling though, when I saw them; I knew, that that's where God was, and that was why He was so far away from me. He was down there with those birds, Lisa, all those beautiful birds that light up like neon colors in the sky. And I thought, if you ever go anywhere Sara, you have to go down there. You have to go to God.

"But later, I knew, Lisa, when I saw that parakeet on my building, that I was wrong. God was up here too. Just sometimes, you can't see Him too clearly. So you have to listen very hard. Or else you'll miss Him. And you won't even know that He was there to begin with."

"Do you think, Sara, that He's here with us right now?"

"Yeah, Lisa, I do. I can see it in that sky over there. In that blue color. I just feel like He's waiting for me to fly right into it, to find my way down south with the rest of those birds. I just know that one day, He's gonna come get me, and that's where I'm gonna wind up."

There she was talking about God. Small little Sara, who

couldn't weigh more than a hundred pounds. With long, shiny, strawberry red hair and so many freckles that her skin looked brown. Sara who would collect spiders in a cup and then let them out in the morning when she could go outside. And she never wanted to go outside. She just wanted to let the spiders out. Sara who talked in a soft voice nobody hardly heard and liked to reach over and hold my hand. Sara, who first shared a kiss with a boy in the sixth grade, when she was eleven, in the closet of a girlfriend's house, playing spin the bottle. She liked it. She wanted to keep playing and playing.

Small little Sara who held my hand that day as we walked outside in the warm air that felt like spring and made me believe there was something out there that I had never caught sight of.

Twenty-Four

It was 9:02 in the morning. Lisa sat by herself and looked at the chalky hospital walls that wrapped around the room, walls filled with tacky posters of Ferris Wheels and roller coasters and boardwalks along the Jersey Shore. They were shabby, in cheap plastic frames, donated, she thought, from some other state agency, probably as they were cleaning out their 1979 wall art collections. That's what this hospital got, she thought as she looked at the walls and the cheap broken tables held together by masking tape. The hospital was supposed to help people feel better, but it seemed carelessly thrown together with all the junk that others didn't want.

As she sat waiting, Lisa thought about all the people who had walked in and out of the rec room before she got there, before she was even born. Sara had been to other hospitals and told her they usually try to push people out the door after about four weeks, regardless of their readiness to leave. There is even a waiting list sometimes.

Waiting lists, she thought to herself. All the times when she felt so alone at school, she never really thought about other people. She heard about suicides, but it never really sunk in; she always felt she was alone in her pain. Now she couldn't stop envisioning people walking in and out of the rec room like a revolving circular door that never stops spinning. How many people have sat on this same chair that she is sitting on now?

She looks around the room at the beige, morbid looking walls and thinks about when she will get out of there. She's been there for a long time.

9:20. Dana's standing outside the glass window, talking to a nurse. Lisa can see her looking in as she finishes her conversation. Then she puts her head down and her hands over her eyes, looking exhausted.

"Okay, girls. I realize I'm late, and I apologize for that," she says rushing into the room. "There was a little matter I had to attend to at the hospital, but, everything is fine now, and I think we should begin. I see the baton is still on the floor. Is there anyone who would like to share something first today?"

There's a thirty-second pause. Then Allison leans back and stretches her arms over her head. "Wow, I'm fucking tired," she yawns. "I couldn't get to sleep last night for shit."

Dana's eyes roll back. "Yes, Allison, did you have something to say? Did you want to go first today?"

Allison, with a furtive smile, leans over and picks up the baton, resting on the edge of her seat. "Well, as a matter of fact, I do. The other day when we were talking about death and what it means to us, I kept thinking about Sara and where she is now."

"And what do you think?"

"I don't know, and I'm kind of freaked out about it."

"Why Allison?"

"Because we really have no way of knowing what happened to her. I mean there could really be a million different things that could've happened, I mean, after she died. But how would we know? None of us would really be able to know. The other day, when we were talking, we all kind of said the same thing, that when we die, we'll feel peace, but we don't really know if that would happen. What if there is nothing, and it's just over?"

Lisa knew Allison was in desperate need of her daily dose of attention. Now it was coming, and though Lisa knew it was better to just sit there and ignore her, she decided to counter her anyway. "So, who gives a shit, Allison? What's your fucking point?"

And just like Lisa had come to know Allison, Allison knew her the same. She could see Lisa was anxious, and a little push in any direction could tip her over. She could tell that about Lisa. And she wanted to tip her over anyway. There was something inside her that just couldn't hold back the temptation to push people over, to see how far she could go, not necessarily out of malice, but just for the thrill, the uncontrollable thrill of knowing she had the power to get under somebody else's skin, anyone else's, whenever she felt like *it. Lisa was just caught up in her path that day. "Yeah, but what if it's not, and what if that heaven and hell Christian thing is right, and we all go to hell for committing suicide? I mean, what if that's where Sara is?"*

And with that idea, something inside lost control. In Lisa's mind, Sara had won by what she did. She was able to do what none of them were able to do successfully, escape. And finding that way out had to mean that things would get better. Sara had to be in a better place, where she could finally lay her head down without unremitting fear wrapping around her mind like a cocoon. And even though she never before did anything violent towards another person, Lisa got up and walked across the circle and pushed Allison so forcefully that her chair fell over, and she fell hard onto the floor. "You fucking cunt," she screamed. "You keep your mouth shut about Sara. Don't you pretend to care. You don't give a shit about anybody.

"You left her there, didn't you? You left her in the woods and let her drive home, and you knew that she wouldn't be all right, just so you could save your fucking ass. It's all about you. Everything you do is just some fucking dramatic hyperbole so you can pull attention towards yourself in any way. Even people you pretend to be friends with, to care about. You just use them and spit them out. I don't believe one fucking word that comes out of your mouth. You fucking probably just made up that whole dramatic story about Adam, just so you would have a fucking way to excuse

your little heroin habit and the reason why you wound up on the street as a whore."

Allison turned around with a delicate smile. After all, she got what she wanted; she was providing a good show, getting that attention she craved like a street cat stumbling upon an unexpected meal. "Fuck you, Lisa. What the fuck do you think you're doing? You don't know me, you fucking loser."

"Both of you sit down."

"Stay out of it, Dana," Allison snapped, ready for it to go further. She looked straight over at Lisa, wiping her brown hair off of her shoulder with her finger tips. "So, what are you gonna do, Lissssaaahhhhh?"

"Okay. Everybody sit down. Now."

Lisa didn't have to think about it. She listened to Dana's warning without hesitation. She knew it wasn't worth going any further. It was a game to Allison, and Lisa didn't want to play. For all her talk about school and people who gave her a hard time, wrote notes on her locker and made up rumors behind her back, Allison really wasn't any different than any of those people she talked about in group, if any of that was real to begin with. Lisa stood there in front of her thinking of all the times she felt badly for Allison, of all the times she listened to her sad stories, and actually felt sorry, would actually go back to her room and pray that Allison would find resolution somehow. Now Lisa looked at her and thought, what a pathetic waste. She wasn't worth any more of her concern, so she just looked over as if she was complying with Dana's instructions and sat down, knowing inside that it wasn't defeat; it was ambivalence for a person who really didn't matter. That's how Lisa wanted it to stay between herself and other people. If she was ever going to pull back the reigns, she would have to take a deep breath and say fuck it. Fuck them all.

Allison, though, wasn't going to give in so quickly. "If you don't watch it, I'm gonna come into your room when you least expect it and slit your fucking throat. Then you can join your little friend Sara."

Lisa looked back. "Fuck you. I'm not afraid of you."

"Allison. What is that supposed to mean?" Dana asked, noticeably shaken. "Sit down," she ordered.

"You fucking make me sick, you bitch. I don't have to sit down or do anything you tell me to."

Lisa looked at Allison, huffing and puffing and making herself go crazy. It would never end with her. Whatever her stories were. Whatever was real or unreal in that little world she created for herself, she would always have the impulse to fuck it up. It wasn't nearly enough for her to play around with the twists and turns in her own life; she had to move it away from herself as well and draw circles and circles of chaos around all those who wandered into her realm. For a moment, Lisa found herself caught up in that web. She thought she had settled it at the horse farm, the last day they were there, when she banished Allison from her world. And she thought she had made it perfectly clear she wasn't interested in her little chitchat or bullshit stories anymore. Now she was coming at her again, taking that web and weaving it around her like a black widow spinning around its prey, with this made up little fable about Sara, the one thing she knew could ignite a flame in Lisa and bring her back into her little diversions.

"You want to slit my throat, Allison? Go for it. I dare you. You think that I'm afraid of you and your little bullshit threats? You're about two-point-two seconds away from them locking you away in that loony bin next door and them keeping you there forever."

"Oh yeah, well you're about two-point-two seconds away from joining that little friend of yours."

"Okay. Both of you sit down." Dana was shaking. She put her hand on Allison to hold her back.

"Get your fucking hands off me, bitch. I don't need to listen to your bullshit no more," Allison said, looking over at Dana with fierce, fiery eyes bulging out of her head like a madman that's finally snapped and is ready to take down anyone in his way.

And Dana can see this in Allison. She is alone with them. No one else is around. If Allison explodes, it would be up to her to restrain her. She tries to reprimand her with her voice, but fear is running through her. And Allison can see every speckle of it, like a spotlight's been lit behind Dana's head, highlighting every drop of sweat along the periphery of her forehead. "Sit down, Allison. I'm not going to tell you twice."

"You're not gonna tell me at all, bitch. You sit down."

"Allison, sit down now. You're under my care. If you don't sit down, I'll have to get someone to restrain you. Amanda." And she looks over, telling Amanda with her anxious eyes to run along and get some help.

"You're not gonna go do anything Amanda, are you?" she says, and Amanda sits there, still, shaking her head back and forth, assuring Allison.

"This is your fault," she said, looking at Lisa. "You little bitch. You just couldn't leave well enough alone. You had to come in here on your high horse making me look weak to everybody else," Allison exclaimed, looking at Lisa with a vast sense of vengeance.

Lisa stood her ground. "I don't know what the fuck you're talking about. You've lost your fucking mind."

And with that trigger, Allison charged over like a bull being released into a great coliseum. Her hands held out firmly, wanting to clamp down tightly around Lisa's fragile neck.

But Dana got between them and forced Allison to the ground, the two of them scrambling around the floor, pulling on each other's hair. Dana struggling to get Allison's arms down to her lower back like she learned during her early training. And Allison screaming and ranting like some malevolent spirit had gotten into her and taken control.

Lisa tried to find an angle where she could sneak in to help

Dana, but before she could figure her way inside, two security guards came charging into the room and quickly pulled the two of them apart, Allison kicking and screaming and punching her arms into the air like she was fighting off some invisible attacker who she just couldn't seem to get off of herself, punching away so hard even the two guards couldn't hold her down long enough to get her arms into a jacket.

When they finally did leave, Dana tried to compose herself, but stumbled backwards, almost falling to the ground, before she caught herself on a chair. She felt weak. Then she stood still for a few moments rubbing her forehead, breathing in deeply to catch her breath. The rest, including Lisa, stood around in silence listening to the hard thump of the clock continue to beat.

But deeper in Lisa, more than in any of the others, a gentle, subdued feeling was filling inside watching the guards pulling Allison's almost lifeless body away. As they took her out of the room, Lisa knew it was for the last time, and an overwhelming sense of relief settled throughout her body.

Part III

Twenty-Five

It's hard to know the sound of a mother's voice when the sound of that voice has been hidden away for so long. And so little girls search and search for voices reading books and telling bedtime stories and singing sweet melodies to baby ears. But sometimes those voices are tucked away too far, and the mind can't trace its steps back to earlier times of comfort.

Now there is a hall, and it's hollow and long and filled with the sound of too many mothers, scared and confused, looking for comfort through the sound of a daughter's voice. They stand, talking to strangers, only those voices and the cold hall between them, but still they cannot see, cannot know what is all around them, and cannot feel the hearts of the lives that were once living inside of them.

Lisa accepted that distance between her and her mother. The ties that once held them together were broken, and the two of them continued to live their lives far away from each other, in two different bodies, in two different worlds; they continued to walk further and further away from anything that may have connected them at one time.

For Lisa, a feeling of love couldn't come back to her. She tried and tried to hear that voice inside of her that said, "I forgive you, Mom," but it just wasn't there. Those sounds just would not come together. So she stayed further and further away, and when her mother called, she wouldn't pick up, and when her mother left messages, she wouldn't respond, and when her mother sat there in front of her in their private meetings with Dana, when it was just the three of them in her office, and Lisa was listening to her superficially talk about her feelings, she sat there and didn't say anything, unable to comprehend the voice that was speaking to her.

"I'm glad the three of us are here again today. There's been a week since you have seen each other, and I would imagine that the two of you thought about what you may want to say to each other during that time. Rosemary, I think Lisa needs to hear from you first. I know that she holds a lot of animosity and resentment towards you. I know that you are aware of that. I want you to tell her how you felt that night when you saw her in your bathroom, so she can see things from your perspective."

Dana wanted Lisa to see how her mother was affected by her attempt to kill herself, and she could see that it was working. She could tell that this thought made it difficult for Rosemary to speak, and Dana had a hope that Lisa would finally be able to see how all of this was affecting her mother, so Lisa would know that her mother really did love her and that her suicide attempt was breaking her on the inside even though she couldn't show it on the outside.

The thought of going back to that moment made Rosemary distant. She looked over to Dana like she hadn't understood what she was saying. Like Dana had asked her a question that was foreign and strange. That there had never been that night. Like her sixteen-year-old daughter had never been minutes away from a death she tried to induce on her own, in Rosemary's bedroom, with her own medication, and a bottle of vodka from her liquor cabinet.

It was two months ago now, almost exactly. Two months and a day. It was 10:00 at night. April was out with her friends. Rosemary and Lisa's father went out at 6:00 that night, Saturday night, for dinner and a movie. That's what they had always done on Saturday night. Sometimes with the girls. Sometimes just the two of them. As April and Lisa got older, it was mostly just the two of them, Rosemary and Tom. April was eighteen and almost finished with high school, much too old to spend a Saturday night with Mom and Dad. And Lisa didn't want to go out with them anymore either. She hadn't in a long time. Rosemary thought it was just her age. Teenage girls don't want to be seen with their parents anymore. When April turned fourteen, it was, "My friends, my friends, my friends, my friends. I don't want to hang out with my mother anymore." When Lisa turned fourteen, she didn't want to talk to her mother anymore either. She didn't seem to want to talk to that many people in general, but Rosemary thought she knew better the second time around. *Just back off. Only a few years. Eventually, when she starts college perhaps, things will change. She'll grow up. She'll want to talk to her mother again.*

The movie was a corny love story with a trite, depressing ending, just the kind of movie Rosemary wanted for a Saturday night. She cried and cried at the ending her husband just thought as ridiculous, but he humored her like he always did and pretended on the way home that he had an actual interest in the plot and that the lead actress was very convincing, Academy Awards nominee. *He would put money on it.*

They got home at 9:58, opened the garage door, and Tom went down to get the mail at the end of the driveway he hadn't picked up in the morning. Rosemary walked in and the lights were on in the kitchen and the living room, and Lisa's schoolbooks were out, but there was no Lisa.

Maybe she went to bed early. Maybe she's on the computer in her bedroom. 10:00 was early for bed on Saturday night, so Rosemary thought she would go in to tell Lisa about the movie. As she walked out of the kitchen and into the hallway to go to the bedroom on the other side of the house, she noticed how everything was dark except for a faint light coming from her bedroom. It was coming from the bathroom. Rosemary thought Lisa had just left it on, or perhaps it was even her before she left to go out. But with each step she took getting closer and closer to the door of her *bedroom, she grew cold and shaky inside. It was as if all of a sudden she knew something was wrong. Like she had just realized she had known something was wrong all night. And this was it. She was going to find out what it was. At first, ideas flashed through Rosemary's head, like she had been in an accident and her life was flashing before her. Maybe someone had broken in. No, no, nothing was wrong like that. The doors were all closed and locked. Maybe something happened in the bathroom. The hairdryer. Water from the sink. Maybe she took a shower and fell and hit her head. Maybe. Maybe. She didn't know what.*

As she got closer and closer, her body got heavier and heavier, and her mind kept thinking, "Oh my God, where's Lisa? Oh my God, what's wrong?" And then she noticed a smell. It smelled like alcohol. Like vodka. Why would it smell like vodka? Was that what Lisa was doing? Drinking in her bedroom. That didn't seem like Lisa.

And then the moment was there. She had to go in. There were no more steps to take in the hallway. She had to go left now and turn into her bedroom. And that's when she saw Lisa, with her head faced down and her body passed out half inside and half outside of her bedroom bathroom. Her body still and the skin on her fingers turning blue.

"How do you think I felt? I saw my daughter turning blue, lying in a puddle of vodka on my bathroom floor. You both think I'm some kind of monster. That I don't have feelings. That I don't

love my daughter. But that's not true. I have feelings."

"I know you do, Rosemary."

"But I have feelings, Lisa. How would you have felt if you saw your baby lying there on the bathroom floor like that?"

"Oh please, Mother. This is about you again."

"Of course it is. It's about me too, Lisa. You're my daughter, and you tried to kill yourself. Of course, I have feelings. You think this is all about you, but I have feelings too. This affects me too. I didn't know what I should do. I didn't know what was happening. I didn't know if I should touch you. Your father came in and called the police, and I couldn't do anything. I just looked at my daughter turning blue, and I couldn't believe that you were going to die right there on my bathroom floor. I didn't know if you were dead already."

"And then what happened, Rosemary?"

"Tom came over and gave her mouth to mouth, but she was still breathing. So he stopped and tried to wake her up and get her to start talking."

"And did that work?"

"A little. He slapped her a couple of times and got her to start talking, but she wasn't really making sense."

"And what did she say when she started talking?"

Rosemary looked at Lisa, directly at her, for the first time in all of their sessions, but when she looked over, Lisa turned away and stared at nothing in the corner of the room. "She said...she kept calling my name. She kept saying, 'Mom, Mom, where are you?' She was calling out for me. Lisa, do you remember that?"

"No."

"That's what you kept saying, Lisa. You kept calling out for me. Like you wanted me there with you."

"I don't believe you."

"But it's true. Ask your father. That's all you kept doing, calling out my name. You don't remember, but I do."

"I don't believe you. I would never call out for you. I know you wouldn't come. You wouldn't come for me when I needed you."

"That's not true. I would come. I would have come if you would have asked. If you would have showed me at all…"

"Fuck you. I hate you so much. You always make things about you. But they're not. This is not about you, Mother. This is about me."

"No, Lisa. This is about both of us. You and me."

"I don't have to listen to this. Throw your own pity party without me. I'm leaving."

But Rosemary got up and stood in front of the doorway and wouldn't let her go.

"What the fuck are you doing? Let me out of here."

"No, Lisa. You're gonna stay here and listen to what I have to say."

"Dana."

"No, Lisa. Look at me, not at her. You think that I don't

have feelings. You think that all of this means nothing to me. That you could have died, and I would have just gone on with my life."

Lisa stood there and looked at her mother with nothing to say.

"You really think I'm such a cold-hearted monster. That all these women that are here today, that they're all like me. That if all of you girls would have died, we would have been okay. We could have just picked up the pieces of our lives and moved on."

"Yes, I do."

"How could you say that to me? I wouldn't have been okay, Lisa. I would never have been okay. You're my daughter. I don't want to see you hurt or in pain, and I could never, never, never be able to handle it if you died, especially, Lisa, if you..."

"If what, Mother? If I killed myself? If I killed myself because I hate you?"

After that was said, there was stillness in the room. It was quiet. Just the ticking of the clock and the foreign, remote voices from outside in the hallway. Lisa turned away and put her eyes under her hands. She didn't know what to do. Something inside felt sorry for the first time, but she didn't want Dana or her mother to see. She could tell what that did to her mother, to send all that blame in her direction, and for the first time, Lisa knew that she didn't mean it. That she didn't mean to hurt her mother so much. She could see what all that hurt was doing; she was breaking her mother the same way she had been broken, and she didn't know how to feel about that. She didn't want to feel sorry, but something inside of her did. And she didn't know how to handle those feelings, so she just walked to the door and left. This time, her mother moved out of the way.

When we have lost the ability to cry,
And our morning opens with expectations of fear,
It is too late to realize
We live within the unclimbable boundaries of
emptiness.

The sensations of movement become too real—
We struggle with the heavy load of our arms
Just to scratch the sensitive skin on our faces.

With eyes looking past our shoulders,
Discolored lips and numb expressions
Melt into polluted urban walls.

And to the ground,
Feet fall deeper in broken concrete
That robs our rhythm and twists our toes.

Pain reminds us that we have to walk.
We cannot collapse
And cause our own demise.

There are still unwanted traces of the unknown,
An uncertain trepidation for a God
That hides behind closed curtains
And graces those who walk through daylight
hours.

In years of illusions,
We watched children run
Under plastic shields of library fiction
Seen only through distant pictures
And thought of hope for rainbows.

In my sky, I know not color.
Only solid images and frozen rain.

Twenty-Six

When Lisa walked out of Dana's office, she imagined the way the cold hallway must have felt under her feet, and she took off her shoes and started to run. She imagined flying off the roof like Sara and how free that must have felt for those few moments in the air. And she thought about being free herself, just like that. She could do it. She could find a place and fly away. Where would that place be, she didn't know. All she knew was what was behind her, all the places she had been, all the people she had known, and how she never wanted to go back. She just wanted to keep running forward, into the blue air that lay in front of her. And fly away. It didn't matter where she would wind up. She just wanted to go.

But Lisa got to the end of the hallway, and there was no place left to go. She had to stop, so she went over to the windows and tried to open each and every one of them. But they wouldn't open passed the two-inch lock that prevented the girls from lifting them. She looked around the room to find something to help her.

"Lisa, what are you doing?"

"No, no, leave me alone. I have to get out of here, Andrea. Help me. Help me find something to lift the window, so I can get out."

"Lisa, you have to be quiet or the nurses are going to restrain you. They're gonna see what you're trying to do. They're gonna take you to the psych ward, just like Allison."

"Then, Andrea, help me. Help me get out of here," she said, still searching frantically, trying to find something to open the window, even though there was nothing to be found.

"Lisa, stop it. Let's go back to your room. We'll talk about it later. We can't talk about it here when everyone is looking at us."

"Andrea, what am I going to do? I can't stay here anymore. I have to leave. Where's Sara? She can help me. She knows how to get out."

"Sara's not here," Dana said quietly.

Lisa stood up and stared out the window, her eyes suddenly fixated on something no one else could see. "Dana, I saw her, in my dream that night. She was flying. And the air was blue with bright little stars that punched holes out of the darkness. She just flew away into the sky. I can still see the softness in her eyes. Her skin is light. And they're not with her. They can't hold onto her anymore.

"Do you think she was going to heaven, Dana? Do you think she could fly away that far?"

Dana wanted to say yes. Yes, Lisa, that's where Sara is, but she couldn't. She just looked at her and cried, cried for the first time *in front of her patients, the little girls she couldn't protect, no matter how much she wanted to. She tried to look for that place where Sara was, but she just couldn't see it. Was that where her father was? Were they in the same place? Why couldn't Dana see it? She prayed and prayed, but God was just an empty space inside of her. A voice she could not hear. Heaven a place she could not imagine. It was just as void and as colorless as the space outside the window that Lisa was staring into, looking for her best friend in a vacuum of emptiness. And Dana realized that emptiness for the first time as she looked across at Lisa and knew she could not help her, knew there would never be words she could find in some textbook that would fill that empty space inside of Lisa and take her misery away. And for the first time, she finally felt close to her father, could almost feel an empathy with a man she tried to hate her entire life. She knew why now, why he couldn't stay here with all that emptiness, even though he must have loved her, even though he probably tried and tried to stay, just for her, but that emptiness was too much to feel.*

She can faintly see his eighteen-year-old eyes as he breaks apart from his mother's embrace the day he leaves for Vietnam. The vivid color in those eyes filled with love for her. A young marine who thought four years, four years, and it will all be over, and I'll look out these same eyes to these same people who love me so much. I'll reach out and touch them, and I'll love them again. Through these same eyes with so much color, so much richness--full of hues just like the ones he saw on the maple trees that stretched out in the distance behind the long tarmac when he boarded the plane to leave the country for the first time. I'll remember those trees, and then I'll dream of America. If I close my eyes, I can feel their cool summer breezes in my mind already.

Dana looked at Lisa and wondered where her tarmac lay, where she would find her spot to fly away, out of this world, out into a distance nobody could see. And she knew why now, and that feeling, that realization, made her numb inside for the first time.

"Where is she? I have to find her. She's in her room. I know she is." Lisa broke away and ran down the hallway to Sara's room, certain she would find her sitting there alone. But there was only a young woman, in her late-thirties at most, standing over Sara's bed, folding her clothes and putting her things into a suitcase. When Lisa walked in, it didn't look like Sara's room anymore. Sara had magazine clippings and half put together necklaces and bracelets she was making with clay beads lying all around the furniture.

Sara loved anything that could fly, so she cut pictures from magazines, of butterflies and birds, and hung them from the ceiling. Dana told the girls to think of things they wanted, to think of things that would make their lives happy, and Sara thought of butterflies and other creatures that lived in the sky. She wanted to be like them, like those butterflies with the pretty wings, she told Lisa. And she wanted a thousand shades of different rainbows on those wings. That was her wish. And she only told that to Lisa. And now when

Lisa ran over to her room, that's what she thought she would find—
Sara and those colorful butterfly clippings hanging from the ceiling.

But Sara wasn't there. Instead, there was a stranger packing
up her things and a garbage can filled with the clippings that used to
decorate this now empty space. Lisa ran to the woman, ripping the
butterflies out of her hand. "What are you doing? Leave her stuff
alone. Who are you? Why are you in Sara's room?" she yelled in a
hard voice.

"Excuse me?"

"Why are you here? What are you doing?" Lisa kept asking.
But she really wasn't talking to her. She just needed someone or
something to be angry with, and the woman was there. "Stop it.
Get out of here. What are you doing with Sara's things? She's
gonna be back. Leave, before she gets here."

"I don't know what you're talking about," the woman said.
"She's not coming back. Sara's not..."

"Stop it. Stop it. You don't know Sara. You don't know
where she is. She's coming back."

"No, Lisa," Dana said behind her, unsure of what she could
do to help. "Lisa, Sara's not coming back. Lisa, Sara's gone."

"No, she's coming back. She's coming back for me. Give me
her stuff and get out of here."

"Lisa, this is Sara's mother. She's packing her things to take
home with her."

"No, she's coming back," Lisa bellowed, unsure of what she

believed. "She has to come back. We have to put the pictures back for when she gets here."

Her mother, now too, was there, standing behind Dana. They all just looked at her, this fragile little girl standing in the middle of Sara's bare room, talking to herself about a life that just didn't make sense, not for so long, and she didn't know how to put the pieces together. She just didn't know how. She didn't know where to begin to start making sense of things. It was easier just to stand there broken.

"Lisa, give Sara's mother her things," Dana said.

"I can't, Dana. I can't let go of her. She was the only sense of peace I ever knew in my life."

"You don't have to, Lisa. You don't have to let go completely."

"Dana, I don't know what I'm supposed to do."

"Come with me, Lisa," her mother said, reaching out for her hand. "I want you to come with me."

And she did. She turned around and took her mother's hand, and she walked out of the room right along side of her.

Tomorrow paints dreamers
In safe suburban suburbs with white picket fences

But she does not show her spectrum of color to me

Tomorrow turns rain clouds into bathing suit weather
With crystal blue sunshine and calming cool breezes

But she does not ease the storms that blow around me

Tomorrow makes children into bright distant dreamers
With eyes fixed over mountains and long gliding rainbows

But tomorrow keeps her pictures blank inside me

Faces filled with today's weary teardrops
Will dry in the dream only tomorrow can bring

But tomorrow, tomorrow, if you will truly be,
You must open that space of dreaming around me.

Twenty-Seven

"Did you write anything in your journal yesterday? Lisa, you don't have to tell me about that. But you have to tell me about something. Anything at all that you're feeling right now or have been feeling this week."

"I wrote a poem."

"About?"

"About tomorrow. About what if I could see tomorrow. What it would look like."

"And what did you find? Did your poem tell you anything?"

"I thought about other people and how they have dreams, how other people talk about tomorrow and what that might look like and how I don't."

"And why do you think that's true, Lisa?"

"Because I thought that I was going to die."

"For how long? How long do you remember feeling like that? Like you wanted to die. Like you wanted to kill yourself."

"I don't know. For a long time. I don't remember exactly when it started."

"Well, do you remember having dreams, do you remember ever thinking of the future and what the future might look like?"

"Yes."

"And what did it look like, Lisa?"

That was the first time she ever felt perfect. Lisa in her eight-year-old mind and her eight-year-old body and her eight-year-old costume that her grandmother made after watching the movie over and over, trying her best to make it look like Dorothy's dress in 1939.

She got everything right that night, all of her lines, all of her stage movements, all of her cues. And she was never nervous. Not like she thought she would be when she was rehearsing the lines in her bedroom at night, over and over and over again, alone in front of the mirror. Then she was comfortable, when she was looking at herself with her own eyes looking back at her. She had practiced on the stage before, but not for real, only during the day when there was no one sitting in front of her. Only empty seats and a vacant gym that was full of sunlight. During those rehearsals, Lisa was unsure how she would feel when those seats were full, and the gym was dark, and she was on that stage alone with only the bright lights ahead of her. What if she forgot her lines or got scared and ran off the stage? What if she did something wrong and people laughed at her? What if everyone laughed? The people from the audience. Her classmates from behind the stage.

She had wanted this role so badly. When she heard they were doing The Wizard of Oz *for her fourth grade play, Lisa knew that she had to be Dorothy. That was it. There was no way that anyone else could play her. It had to be Lisa. So she watched the movie, over and over and over and over, and she got the script, and she read it with her mother, over and over and over again, and she practiced singing "Somewhere Over the Rainbow" with her grandfather playing the piano for help, until she knew her voice sounded just right. And it did. All the help. All the practice. It worked. She sang just like Dorothy did in Kansas, only half of Judy Garland's age, but her voice sounded almost as smooth and as glowing as in the film.*

She didn't know for a week, and she was scared. She couldn't eat, and she couldn't sleep. Eight years old and Lisa was nervous for the first time. If she didn't get the part, what would she do? She couldn't stand watching another one of her classmates in a role she knew should be hers. Every morning in class, when she saw her teacher looking at papers, she thought this would be the day. She's going to read off one of those papers and tell the class who would play what part in the play. Every day, she had to wait. Monday. Tuesday. Wednesday. Thursday. And then Friday. And there was that piece of paper with Dorothy's name on it, and Lisa's name right beside it.

And she never got scared on that stage. Actually, she felt stronger than ever. She felt alive. She felt like something was actually right inside of her. And she recited her lines perfectly, almost like she was Dorothy herself, and for a brief moment, stronger and longer than ever really before or ever really after, Lisa felt happy. And she remembers and remembers and remembers that.

"I always thought I would be happy, I guess, but who doesn't? When I saw myself as an adult, I saw myself being happy. I saw myself with a husband, and we never fought, and we had two children, and we went on vacations a lot. I always wanted to go on vacations a lot with my husband."

"And what else, Lisa? What about for you? What did you see yourself doing with your life?"

"I wanted to be an actress, Dana. That's what I wanted to do. I did it when I was little, and I really liked it. I acted in a play once, and I was actually the lead. I was Dorothy in *The Wizard of Oz*. And I was really good. And I convinced my mom to let me go to acting school, and I did it. I went until I was twelve."

"And why did you stop going if you liked it so much."

"I don't know. Everything started falling apart in my life."

"Why Lisa?"

"Because, I don't know, Dana. Everything started getting so hard. I mean, it wasn't so hard before that."

"What started getting so hard, Lisa? You were only twelve-years-old. What started getting so hard?"

"I hate when people talk to me like that."

"Like what, Lisa?"

"Like I'm so young, so I shouldn't have any problems. But your life is different. You forget how it was when you were in high school. How you can be so trapped when you're there. Like you have no way out."

"Tell me about it, Lisa. Why did they make you feel trapped when you were only twelve?"

"Because I started losing my friends, Dana. I don't know what happened. Before that, I was all right. I had friends. I remember being happy when I was younger, I do. I say that I don't, but I do. I remember having birthday parties and going to sleepovers and going on trips with my family and going fishing and acting and having fun. I remember those things, I do. But it's like things got so bad afterwards that none of that mattered anymore."

"How did things get bad, Lisa?"

"I started getting ugly. I know you don't want to hear it, but it's true. The girls around me started getting pretty, but I didn't. I kept gaining weight, and my skin got so gross. And there was nothing I could do about it. And the girls around me, their breasts started to grow, and their hair got pretty, and none of that started happening to me."

"Did you ever think that you're a type of late bloomer? That maybe one day you would be pretty too, like maybe some of those things would change?"

"Yes, but they didn't. They just kept getting worse. And it wasn't just me. It wasn't just that I had to live with myself, under my own skin. Everybody else had to look at me, and they made me know I wasn't like them. None of the boys would talk to me. I mean, even if I just tried to say things to them or ask a question or something, they would walk away like they were embarrassed. And sometimes they would even make fun of me. Make fun of me with somebody else because I was trying to talk to them. And it's not like I was trying to flirt. I would just say something stupid, and then it started to catch on that Lisa Scanavan was someone that nobody wanted to talk to. And I lost more and more friends, for nothing, for no reason. By the time eighth grade was over, I just felt so awful about myself. I felt like nobody was ever gonna like me again."

"Is that when you quit acting school?"

"Yes." And as she said that, Lisa started to cry, remembering a thought of a dream that was once so real to her. She wanted it so badly, and she was sure that was what her life would look like. That she would be an actress. That she would be popular. That she would be strong. That she would have friends. And that she would be loved. But none of that happened. Dream after dream after dream had died, and she just couldn't take living like that any longer. She couldn't let all of them win and use her as their power, as their method of making themselves look good, while she was dying. While she was dying every day. It had to come to an end, and that had to be her goal. That was the only thing she could hold onto when other people around her laughed or told jokes in her face or purposely left her to be the last one to be called for a team in gym class. "This is going to be over soon. I promise," she kept telling herself.

"Lisa, do you think that all people are like that?"

Now, she couldn't stop crying. The tears came so hard that she found it difficult to talk through them. "Dana, I don't know. I don't know anything else. All I know is the way they made me feel. I can't explain how horrible it is when everybody laughs at you."

"This is why, Lisa, that I push you towards your mother all the time, even though you don't want to hear it, even though you blame her."

"Why, Dana? I don't understand."

"Because you need your family, Lisa. You need them as support when times are bad, and it seems like everyone is against you. You need them to be your rock.

"Lisa, I didn't have that, and I've felt vulnerable all my life."

"Because your father died in the war?"

"Yes, he died, Lisa. Both him and my mother are dead. But you have a chance to make things better with your family. You have a chance that I never had.

"Lisa, what did you and your mother talk about the other day, when you were alone? Do you want to tell me?"

"Do I have a choice?"

"Yes, Lisa. You always have a choice. That's what I have been trying to tell you. This is your life. You get to make the decisions."

"What if I don't know what to decide? What if I don't

know where to go?"

"Then you just take it day by day and wait for the answers to come to you. Don't feel overwhelmed, Lisa. Just calm down and wait for the answers to come, always knowing that you have the time to make your own decisions, and you have the power to make them too. You have the power to decide what you want to do with your life and whom you want to do it with. You never have to be around people you don't want to be around, Lisa. You never have to feel like you're being trapped again."

"So what do you think I should do now?"

"Well, what do *you* think you should do? Isn't that the point of this conversation?"

"I guess."

"Well, what do you think you should do, Lisa?"

"I'm not going to go to school. That's what we talked about the other day. I told her that I didn't want to go back to school, even to St. Pat's, and she said that was okay. That she would pay for me to get homeschooled instead."

"And how does that make you feel?"

"Relieved. It makes me feel really relieved that I never have to go back to that school again, and I never have to see any of those people. She said I never have to. That she would even go and clean out my locker. That I didn't have to go with her."

"And what about the other school? You didn't want to try going back to that one either?"

"No, I'm afraid to do that, Dana. Going back to another school just makes me so afraid. I can't even breathe when I think about it, but when she said I didn't have to go back there, back to any school, I felt safe for the first time since I can remember. Is that strange? I've felt so anxious and sick inside for years, and when I knew I didn't have to go back to school, I felt like everything was starting to relax in me."

"It's not strange, Lisa. All of your pain, it all came from being there. Soon, the longer that you are away, you'll see that you'll feel protected. And you'll know what happiness is like again."

Twenty-Eight

The elders say, a long, long time ago, there lived a beautiful bird, unlike any other, who lived in a magical forest surrounded by giant mountains, so lofty they guarded the valley against the creatures who lived outside of them. But also so enormous that the animals couldn't get out. The air was murky and poisonous at certain altitudes, and even the younger, more curious birds were forced to learn the lessons that so many of their elders had in the past. It was impossible to escape, and the only chance they had for happiness was to find contentment in their own little piece of the world.

Rose Petal was different, and all the other birds in the village knew it from the time her egg was hatched. As soon as her little shell started cracking, it seemed like her wings were ready for flight, and whereas it took the other birds months and months for their feathers to grow colors, Rose Petal's wings were already a radiant mixture of scarlet and gold by the time she flew out of her shell, so the other birds knew that something was different right from the beginning. Her mother, Raven Tail, had never been married, and though the females of the flock speculated and speculated who could be the male that fertilized Raven's eggs, they never thought that Raven Tail could be so bold as to mate with the sun god, Helios, until they saw Rose Petal's wings. Mating with the gods, of course, was strictly forbidden, and so the birds punished both Raven Tail and Rose Petal by making them live far away and treating them like outcasts.

All of this spiteful treatment from the other birds was hard on Raven Tail, and when Rose Petal was very small, she cried and cried so much that she drowned herself in a puddle of her own tears, leaving Rose Petal to grow up all alone, with no parents and with no friends.

When Rose Petal was old enough to feel loneliness, she flew into town, determined to make friends with some of the other young birds; but whenever they saw Rose Petal, the young birds quickly tried to frighten her and did everything they could to make her run away, including calling her names that made her feel ugly and throwing heavy things at her like rocks and wood. This was too much for Rose Petal, and after a few attempts, she decided not to go into town anymore; instead, she would stay in her own nest and wait for death to take her like it did for her mother.

But it seemed like death had forgotten about Rose Petal as well, for it never found her, and so Rose Petal waited and waited, alone and afraid, for five hundred long years. On her five hundredth birthday, she couldn't wait any longer, so she gathered little pieces of wood and little pieces of glass, any that she could find throughout the forest, and built a funeral pyre in her own nest. As Rose Petal lay there waiting for it to catch fire, the pieces of glass caught the reflection of the sun, and suddenly Helios looked down and saw what his daughter was trying to do. Frightened, he tried desperately to break the barriers of the sky. But he was too late and was forced to watch as the nest caught fire, and Rose Petal ignited, her gold and scarlet feathers burning into flames and extinguishing the life she had known in the forest.

Without delay, Helios ordered the wind and the sky to bring Rose Petal back to life and suddenly a new bird appeared through the blackness of the ashes. Sad and distraught and not wanting to go on again through another life of loneliness, Rose Petal stayed in her nest crying until a ball of light appeared in front of her.

"Rose Petal, I am your father, Helios," the ball of light said. "All of these years, the mountains would not let you free because they were afraid if you crossed over to the land of people, they would not be ready for your powerful beauty. But now I have come to help you. Fly into my light, and when you reach the top of the mountain, I will protect you, and when you fly over to the other side, you will be free. You will have another life in a new world with other animals and living people. There you will bring the joy of flight and majesty to other creatures, and they will worship you. If you are ever afraid again, build yourself another nest made of glass and wood and light your body into flames. The wind and the sky will come to you once more and help you start anew."

And so Rose Petal did what Helios said, and as she passed over the mountains, she could smell the aroma of unpolluted air and hear the gentle music of people laughing and feel the soothing beat of their dances. The people, in turn, saw the scarlet bird and gave thanks and praise to the heavens for sending them such a beautiful gift. The songs that Rose Petal heard were actually dedicated to her arrival, and the people of the land forever praised their new deity and gave her another name. From then on, Rose Petal was known as the

Phoenix, and her new life was to be filled with happiness, for the people saw her as a chance for hope and renewal and painted Rose Petal's being with glory and veneration, making her feel at peace for the first time since she was born.

Epilogue

He raped a nine-year-old girl. Seventeen years later, he put his head down in his Firebird. Or so she read, when she was trying to figure out her father's suicide.

That's what she learned, the first time she opened the note, having the strength to do it after a night of heavy drinking her freshman year of college. All those muffled sensations helped her stay calm and focused as she read this iceberg of her father's young life. It was her drunkenness that made her finally understand that little brown pouch with his heroin vial. It was there in that box she kept with the other little memories of his life. A small leather pouch with a burned up metal spoon and an overused needle. They gave it all to her when she was only fifteen-years-old. But she wanted to see a brightness in his memory, so she put it all away and left his note sealed up in its tiny white envelope.

She knows fluently about PTSD from scholarly textbooks and a graduate dissertation, but still she thinks, how can a man not remember? His mind moves him away, slowly, from the truth, but the truth is still there, however deeply it lay under hardened mud and yearly debris that cake on top of it, like the ground that nourishes an old cedar box in a carefully maintained cemetery. On top, neatly organized white crosses, lines and lines of them, that seem to lie across an infinite stream of land. And the grass that grows back every year, smelling fresh and crisp like the yard of a baseball field. But underneath, there are still those boxes, filled with the fleshless remains of dead soldiers who can no longer move or think or feel. And they remain, just like the memories of old men who see their pasts in broken images of lives they once lived, pretending they were the heroes they imagined as children listening to stories told by graying librarians in kindergarten classes. Then, they believed that soldiers won medals and that war encompassed a clear line that divided good from evil. The dividing line was vivid and distinct, and those who survived would come home with a comforted feeling of moral resolution. At twenty-two, that line became wavy and distorted and mostly ambiguous, and the side he was standing on as a soldier was gray and muddied, and he no longer understood the difference between black and white in his own soul. That was the only way to make sense of it, his daughter thought, after she opened the note. The distinction was lost. Too many burning villages he helped to ignite. Too many landmines he watched his friends walk over. Too many snipers hidden under the lush canopy of the jungle.

He once held a Bible in his hands. He once walked to the top of a mountain to find the grace of God. He walked and he walked, and in that gentle humid air, he could feel the presence of the Lord fill his body. Surely, He would walk with him again through the fields he had never seen. Surely, there was a mountain he could find in Vietnam where God would be waiting. But God wasn't there. Only the hard, darting sounds of AK-47s and black market Uzis that came out of nowhere and killed the only goodness he ever remembered. What was life now? How did it go on? It was unclear. Like the line he once saw between good and evil. Now it was only rain soaked mud in jungles that rained too much to show their beauty. And the voices of little children, that brought him back to that tenderness he once felt when he walked on that mountain. When he saw her, she must have reminded him of that tenderness so much, too much, that he couldn't keep himself away. If he could just feel her, once, from the inside, then maybe that feeling of God sinking into his pores would come back to him, and he would no longer hear the hard sounds of war.

She had to make it pure. She had to rescue the memory of her father from the demons that buried his soul in Vietnam.

Just like he had to lay his head down in that Firebird, so he could no longer hear the voices of the dead children. That's what Dana realized. The only thing she could do to make sense of her own father's life. He had to. And now, as a young doctor, she heard voices of her own and understood him for the first time. But they were alive, and they weren't children, and she needed to save them.

One of them, she lost already, but it wasn't a voice she heard. It was a picture she saw of Sara flying off the roof into the starry-lit sky. In this image, she never falls. The air opens up and catches her before she can fall to the ground and gives Sara the peace she wasn't strong enough to provide. She is cradled there forever, spread out through the nighttime sky. When she looks up, she can see her lying there among the stars. The girl who could fly, she tells herself.

It would be easy to let the others go, like she let the memory of her father lay safe behind the talisman of a Marine Corps Expeditionary Medal, all hardened and heroic, sitting on top of her fireplace mantle. But could she do that now? Could she just walk away and let the demons come back to strangle the life out of Lisa and Amanda, Allison and Andrea, if she just quit, like she was thinking about tonight in her office, smoking too many cigarettes and looking through the notes she had written about the girls. Their lives were in her hands. And she lost one of them already. In only four weeks. Sara, who lives in the sky.

Every day she would awaken with the horror that her most terrible fear would come to be. That even if she saved them, she could never save them. Like her father could never be saved. Even when back to the safety of his country, the realities of war would never leave. The past was something he would carry through his life until he was compelled to end it. And their pasts too, she often thought, would follow the girls at a close distance they could never escape from.

It would be easier for her to walk away. To leave her notes spread out on her desk for a replacement to pick up. One that was more qualified to treat them. She couldn't let another person die under her watch, to know that it was her fault. Either she would leave, or she would have to protect them.

She was their line now. The only image that separated their childhood memories of carefree days and mothers who would never hurt them from the shadowy landscape of their high school walls, wrapping around them like the nighttime sky in the eyes of a young marine. When they moved out into their own darkness, what would lie before them? Would she have armed them with the tools they needed to survive or would she have failed them like she had done before, to her father and to Sara?

Denise Dragiewicz

T'was Grace that brought us safe thus far,

and Grace will lead us home.

ABOUT THE AUTHOR

Denise Dragiewicz taught writing at the collegiate level for over a decade, including Hofstra University and the University of Alaska. She studied creative writing at Rutgers University and at the Paris American Academy in France. Currently, she works as a documentary film director with a special emphasis in environmental films. *The People Could Fly*, her debut novel, uses a variety of literary strategies to depict a unique perspective of life in contemporary America.

www.denisedragiewicz.com